HOGAN'S BUNCH

The Winnemucca Kid is a wild buckaroo with unorthodox ways of busting banks, but when he and his doxy, Della, join Dan Hogan's bunch of bungling bandits, things start to go wrong. The Wyoming governor has raised a super-posse to smoke the robbers out of their roosts, and when the Kid kidnaps a feisty young cabaret artiste, things certainly hot up. It all turns to tragedy when one of Hogan's stray bullets kills the wife of a young greenhorn, Jed Long, who vows vengeance.

JACKSON DAVIS

HOGAN'S BUNCH

Complete and Unabridged

LINFORD
Leicester

First published in Great Britain in 2000 by
Robert Hale Limited
London

First Linford Edition
published 2001
by arrangement with
Robert Hale Limited
London

British Library CIP Data

Davis, Jackson, *1937 –*
Hogan's bunch.—Large print ed.—
Linford western library
1. Western stories
2. Large type books
I. Title
823.9′14 [F]

ISBN 0–7089–4560–0

Published by
F. A. Thorpe (Publishing)
Anstey, Leicestershire

Set by Words & Graphics Ltd.
Anstey, Leicestershire
Printed and bound in Great Britain by
T. J. International Ltd., Padstow, Cornwall

This book is printed on acid-free paper

1

'Business sure is slack today.' Hyram G. Winterbottam, manager of the First National Bank at Rapid City, Dakota, adjusted his celluloid collar and called across to his clerk. 'It's nearly four. You ready to lock the safe?'

Hank Thompson, the elderly bank guard, stirred from his daydream of more exciting days, eased his backside on the uncomfortable chair, and gripped hold of the shotgun across his knees. It sounded like they were going to have an early night. They hadn't had a customer all afternoon.

'Hang on, sir,' the clerk said. 'There's somebody coming in.'

All three watched as the brass handle of the big oak door was turned, and the hinges creaked as it was slowly pushed open. There was a pause. And a mule put its head through, waggling its ears enquiringly. Somebody must have given it a whack on the rump, for it started forward, skittered up to the grille, bared its yellow teeth, and gave an ear-piercing, honking bray.

'What the devil?' Winterbottam pointed at the beast. 'There's a note pinned between his ears.'

Hank Thompson scrambled to his feet, thumbed back the hammers of his shotgun, and swung it towards the half-open door. 'Whoever's out there, you better be ready,' he shouted. 'I'm comin' out with both barrels smoking.'

'Just a minute, Hank,' Hyram snapped. 'See what the note says first.'

As befitted a former soldier, Indian fighter, pony express rider, and sheriff, Hank kept his eyes on the door and backed up towards the mule. He reached out, took the piece of card-board tucked in its head-strap, and handed it through the grille.

HOWDY GENTS — PUT EVRI DOL-LUR YOO GOT IN MI SADDUL BAGS QUICK. THERE'S A BOTTUL OF NITROGLIZZENIN HANGIN ROUND MY NECK. YOO MAKE ONE FOLSE MOOV I'M GONNA BLOW US ALL TO KINGDUM KUM!

In a faltering voice the clerk read out the ill-spelt message and quavered, 'There *is* a bottle, sir.'

'Nitroglycerine?'

'It could be,' Hank Thompson said. 'There's that copper mine outside town. Looks like there's some kinda fuse leading outa the door. Maybe I can dismantle it.'

'No!' Hyram Winterbottam screamed. 'Don't touch it!'

The mule snorted and stared at them impatiently, as if waiting to be attended to. The fuse wire was wound around a rope that whoever it was outside appeared to be holding. Hank had the idea he was watching them through the crack in the door hinge.

'You'll never git away with this,' he shouted.

'Sir, there's a postscript on the other side,' the clerk said, and read out, ' 'Hurry up, I ain't got all day. Do not try to leave the bank for at least five minutes after I have gone. Or else. Thank you. Have a nice day.' It's signed, Hee Haw.'

'Careful,' Hyram Winterbottam cautioned. 'The slightest untoward movement and we could all go up. How much have we got in the safe?'

'Seven hundred and fifty-nine dollars, sir.'

'Get it out. Put it in the saddle-bags. Back off, Mr Thompson. There's nothing we can do.'

Hank Thompson reluctantly backed off and watched as the young clerk brought wads of greenbacks and stuffed them into a pair of saddle-bags slung over the mule's back. 'I'll hold the brute steady,' he growled. 'Mr Winterbottam's right. We're hogtied. We don't want no funerals.'

'Give him the change, too,' Winter-bottam whimpered, shoving it through the grille. 'Get him out of here.'

'OK,' Hank bellowed. 'We sendin' out all we got. You can have it.'

There was a jerk on the rope from outside. The mule braced its neck, resisting, but then complied, and moved docilely towards the door, nosing out through it. The door slammed shut, and the three occupants of the bank stared at each other.

'I'll go git him,' Hank gritted out.

'No.' The manager mopped his brow with relief. 'Give him five minutes like he said. The sheriff can raise a posse, get on his trail.'

Outside the bank, a handsome half-breed, dressed in range leathers, grinned as he greeted the mule and scooped the saddle-bags from his back. 'Well done, ol' fella.' He took the bottle of clear liquid from his neck and pulled away the rope and fuse, tossing them aside. He placed the bottle on the bank stoop.

There were few people about to take much notice of what he was doing, a couple of women gossiping outside the post office, a homesteader loading up his wagon at the general store. A butcher in his shop opposite was sharpening his knife, and appeared to be the only one watching what was going on.

'Now you hightail it outa town.' The cowboy raised his boot and raked his spur across the mule's backside, hard. The animal set off, kicking his heels, braying his anger and pain, and went at a stiff-legged trot out past the sheriff's office and the church. He had always been a keen runaway, and, with any luck, would keep going for five miles or so until he found a patch to graze. 'So long, pardner.'

The 'breed, in his high-crowned Stetson and fringed chaps, hurried at a jog-trot across the dusty street, jumped on to the sidewalk and disappeared into the lobby of the town hotel.

In a room directly above, a near-naked girl in a narrow iron bed raised herself as the cowboy burst in.

'Hiya, Kid. What you been up to?'

'Nuthin' much.' The Winnemucca Kid, as he was known, smiled. 'Jest tryin' to raise me a loan from the bank.'

'You comin' back to bed?'

'Nope. I gotta be on my way, Della.' He raised a half-empty bottle of bourbon to his lips and winced as he swallowed. He picked up a Winchester carbine propped against the wall and went to the window. He poked the barrel through the curtain and watched. The bank door was being cautiously opened. Old Hank Thompson showed himself with his shotgun, and froze when he saw the bottle of nitroglycerine. He glanced about and reached a hand, cautiously, to pick it up.

The Winnemucca Kid expertly levered the Winchester, took aim, and cracked out a shot. It whistled past Hank's head and splintered into the door. The guard whipped his hand away from the bottle and jumped back inside.

'What in tarnation you playing at?' Della rolled from the bed, dressed only in a pair of skimpy cotton drawers and black stockings held up by red garters. 'You nearly made me jump out of my skin.'

The Kid put an arm around her slim, warm waist and kissed her upturned lips. 'Mmm, honey, you're a cutey,' he murmured. 'I wish I had time to stay.'

'Where you going, Kid? Can't I come, too? I ain't got nuthin' here to stay for. Take me with you.'

'Sorry, Della. No can do. I gotta move fast.' He took a hundred-dollar bill from the saddle-bag. 'Here, that 'bout covers what I owe you.'

'A hundred? Wow! I never seen one of these afore.'

'Yeah, you better wait awhile 'fore you change it. So long.' He went to the window at the back of the room, put a foot on the sill.

'When will I see you again?'

'I'll be around.' He ducked through, jumped down on to the roof of an outhouse and on to the back of his waiting pinto. He set off at a canter away from the houses in the opposite direction to the way the mule had gone.

Della stood watching the bank-robber disappear in a haze of dust across the plain in an arrow-straight line towards the north-east. 'Don't leave me, Kid,' she cried. 'You rotten bastard.'

Over at the bank Hank Thompson stood away from the door. 'I make a move out there he's gonna do what he threatened, blow us all to hell.'

'Come on, man,' Winterbottam said. 'We'll get out the back window and go get the sheriff.'

Some minutes later the local lawman, Ned Hagen, the bank staff, and a small band of citizens hurried back down the street. The butcher shouted across from his door, pointing after the mule, 'He went thataway.'

The sheriff carefully picked up the

bottle of nitro, removed the stopper, let a tiny drop spill on to the dust, and jerked his head back as it exploded with a hissing cloud and a small hole appeared in the dirt road. 'Wow! This is the real thang.'

Hank pointed to the hotel window. 'He took a shot at me from up there. Jest to warn me off, I guess.'

'Yeah, well you're lucky you didn't go up in smoke.' The sheriff carefully re-stoppered the bottle, placed it aside and led the way across. 'Let's take a look.'

Della was buttoning her blouse when Sheriff Hagen and the others burst in. She jumped back in fright.

'What do you want?'

'Where is he?'

'Gawn.'

'Which way?'

She stared at them, wide-eyed and pointed the way the mule had gone. 'South.'

Hyram Winterbottam approached her and whipped her knickers open. He groped inside and pulled out the hundred-dollar bill. 'I'll have this, you little hoo-er. It don't belong to you.'

Hagen pushed her back on the bed. 'I'll talk to you later. C'mon, men, we'd better git after him. Who's gonna ride with me?'

The sheriff could raise only seven men for his posse, including old Hank. 'You coming with us?' he shouted at the butcher, who, in his bloody apron, was removing a carcass hanging outside his shop.

'Nope. I'm too busy.' The butcher was a balding, bullet-headed man, sturdily built. 'I got a lot of orders to meet. I ain't got time to go chasing round the country.'

Hagen glowered at him and spat, contemptuously. 'You mean you're too yeller,' he growled.

'We're wasting time,' Hank Thompson said. 'Let's git.'

The butcher watched them go racing out of town. 'Durn fools.' He carried the carcass inside, flicked away buzzing flies, tossed it in a wire-mesh food-safe. He whipped off his apron, put a derby hat on his head, went out back, saddled a bay horse, and swung into the saddle. 'Yaugh!' he cried and set off across the blue sage in the opposite direction to that of the posse.

'Men!' Della stormed, as she buttoned a bolero jacket and shook her long skirt straight over her leather boots. 'Damn cheek they got. That hundred-dollar bill was mine. I earned it.'

She had her pony hitched outside and had been planning to return to Madame Rosie's parlour house on the edge of town. 'I sure am sick of dumb cowhands maulin' me. If they was all like the Kid it'd be different.'

Della looked out of the window and saw the broad-backed butcher in his bowler hat heading away on horseback towards the north-east. 'Where's he going to?' She pursed lips over her rather full teeth, which gave her face a hard, determined look. 'He goin' after him?'

She went downstairs and climbed up, awkwardly, to ride side-saddle on the pony, in accordance with female fashion 'If *he* can, *we* can, too. Sod Madame Rosie.' She headed her mount out of town and at a fast jog followed the spiral of dust the butcher's horse had kicked up. As soon as she was out of eyeshot she hoicked up her skirt and petticoat and rode astride, more comfortably. 'That's better,' she said. 'They won't get away from us.'

2

'Oh, bury me not on the lone prairie,' Winnemucca was hollering. 'Where the wild coyotes will howl over me.'

He fed his small fire with what dry kindling he could find in the gulch of cottonwoods where he had made camp for the night, and tended a skinned jack rabbit roasting on a spit.

'Yoodle-lady . . . yoodle-la-hady . . . yoodle-yee!'

It was early summer and a good time of year to be sleeping under the stars. It was great to be free once again, most of his young life spreading out in front of him, free to ride his bronc wherever he chose. And it was a snug feeling to have become rich so easily. Well, not exactly rich, but seven hundred dollars was a lot of moolah to him. His pinto had carried him a good distance from Rapid City and he had cantered on in the afterglow of the sunset until he had reached the creek. He had little care of the posse catching up. 'Them dumb-clucks ain't got a clue,' he laughed. He would get a few hours' rest and head on before sun-up.

At least, he thought he would. He had made himself comfortable — rolled up in his blanket, nestling on his saddle by the fire, his hat over his eyes, when he felt the touch of cold iron against his temple. He looked up, and, by the light of the flames, saw the Rapid City butcher grinning at him.

'I ain't gonna bury you on no lone prairie. I'll leave you to be made supper of by them wild coyotes you been howlin' about.' The butcher jerked the blanket back and removed the Kid's nickel-plated Allen and Hopkins .36 from its holster, tossing it into the bushes. 'Just hand me that pair of saddle-bags you got under you. Nice an' easy now.'

'How the hell you creep up on me?' Winnemucca asked. 'Like some durn lousy redskin?'

'Well, son, you weren't too difficult to locate with all your caterwaulin'. And ain't you got Injun blood in you? You shoulda heard me coming. Come on, boy, do as I say. I don't want to have to kill you.'

'Keep your hair on, mister. What little you got.' Vivid blue eyes in the dark planes of his face were illumined by the firelight. He reached a hand behind his back for the saddle-bags, jerked them free, and kept up the momentum, clouting the butcher a stinging blow across his face. At the same time he kicked out, sending the butcher sprawling. There was a flash of fire from the man's new-fangled automatic revolver, and a slug scorched the Kid's cheek and whined away.

'You would, would you?' The Kid leaped to his feet and thrashed the man with the heavy leather satchels. Again, a shot spat out, hissing past his head. 'You're gittin' me mad, you lousy bushwhackin' thief.'

'Wait a minute.' The man on the ground fended off the blows with his arms, waving his revolver about. 'I'm on your side. I sent the posse off on a wild goose chase.' He now had the Krug automatic pointed dangerously at the Kid's chest. 'Let's talk about this.'

'Yeah.' The Winnemucca Kid backed warily away. 'What's to talk about?'

'I got the drop on you, ain't I?' The butcher got to his feet. 'I could take you back. Or I could shoot you, keep that cash.'

'Here.' The Kid scowled and tossed it down. 'You can have it.'

'No. What's the point? I wouldn't be able to sleep nights thinkin' you were after me, creepin' up in the night with that knife of yours. I like your style, Kid. What I'm sayin' is we split this cash half-ways. I'm tired of going straight. I'm ready to join you on your next heist. Two guns is better than one. How about it?'

'Partners?' The Kid sized up his opponent. He was a good three or four stone heavier and built like a rock. He knew he didn't have much chance in a brawl. 'I dunno,' he mumbled, 'I'm a loner.' He stooped to pick up his Stetson and at the same time snatched hold of a burning log from the fire and hurled it into the butcher's face. As the man recoiled, knocking the log away, the Kid slammed his left fist into his abdomen. It was like hitting a brick wall.

'So that's how you want it?' The butcher grinned, wiping burning ash from his face. He tucked the automatic into a shoulder holster, gave a roar like a rutting buffalo, and threw himself on the younger man. They went at it hammer and tongs with flailing fists, but Winnemucca, a slim ten stone, was getting the worst of it. He went down as a ham-sized knuckle hammered into his nose. The Kid found himself pinned to the ground on the receiving end of more blows to the head.

'OK,' he cried. 'I've had enough.'

In the excitement of the fight the

butcher hadn't noticed the girl arrive on her pony. 'You better believe it,' he grunted, giving him another smack to the jaw.

'Uhh!' The butcher's eyes glazed over as a Winchester hammered across the back of his skull, and he succumbed into unconsciousness.

'What the hell you doin' here, Della?' Winnemucca asked, as he rolled the recumbent man from him.

'You looked like you could do with some help. I took this out your saddle boot.'

'Yeah, well, thanks.' The Kid stumbled to his feet, holding his head back, trying to stop the blood flow. 'I believe he's broke by dose.'

'Can you breathe through it?'

The Kid snorted, deeply. 'Duh, yeah.'

'So it ain't broke. You're lucky. That big bully was about to beat you to death.'

'It was my fault. I shoulda played square.' He went to the brook and splashed his bruised face. 'You didn't answer my question.'

'Aw, I'm tired of whorin'. I wanna ride with you. Seems you need someone to look after you.'

'That ain't a good idea, Della. Once you cross the line there ain't no goin' back.'

'What I got to go back to? Me, my brothers, we already gone to the bad. Come on, Kid, be a sport.'

'I s'pose, seein' as you've come so far, you might as well ride along. But get this straight, I ain't the marryin' kind. I'm a free man. Don't you try ropin' me.'

'Doncha worry about that. My Ma and Pa put me off ever wantin' to marry anybody.' Nonetheless, in spite of her bravado, the young woman looked at him rather wistfully. 'I'll jest do whatever you want.'

'Let's tie this bustard up.' The Kid took his lariat and hogtied the butcher, pinning his arms, wrists and ankles as he began to come round. 'Who the hell are you, mister?'

'What hit me?' The butcher blinked his eyes. 'Where am I? Who's she?'

'I'm sorry, pal. We weren't evenly matched. I needed some assistance. We're gonna leave you here. I guess the posse will find you 'fore the buzzards do.'

'Aw, come on. I coulda killed you. But I gave you a chance. I'm a man of my word.'

'Too bad,' Winnemucca sniffed. 'Look what you done to my nose. Get some coffee brewin', Della Rose.'

'Good idea. Ain't I seen her in Rapid City?'

'Yeah, an' you're the butcher.'

'Thass right. Bill Laverty, prime cuts and home-cooked hams. I'm kinda tired of that trade. I jest done two years in Wyomin' state prison. I'm on parole and sworn to be on good behaviour. But, hell, butcherin' don't pay enough. Come on, I like you. Be a pal. Cut me free. We can be partners, like I said.'

The Kid pouted his lips which were already beginning to puff up from the blows. 'I like the way you show you like somebody. Try to make mincemeat of their face.'

'Yes, you big oaf,' Della cried. 'You coulda ruined his looks.'

'Yeah.' The Kid made a down-turned grimace. 'He was probably jealous.'

There was a touch of conceit to the way he tossed back his shoulder-length hair, black and shimmering as a crow's wing, away from the copper planes of his part-Indian face, his mouth turned in a crooked smile. He knew he was a handsome young devil who turned girls' eyes. 'He's so durn ugly he just wanted to ruin me.'

'Aw, cut it out. We're two of a kind. Where you headin' Kid? I'll come with you.'

'You'd like to know, eh? What's your name? Laverty? Well, I ain't so sure I believe you. And I sure don't need no pard. I got this damn prairie nymph invited herself along as it is.'

'Yes,' Della put in. 'Two's company. Three ain't.'

The Kid squatted on a log and sipped at a tin cup of hot black coffee which she handed him as he studied the bound older man. 'Moon's fit to rise. Come on, Della. We're gittin' outa here. I don't trust this fella. What's he following me around for, anyhow?'

Della was flittering her fingers through Laverty's pockets with the practised ease of one in her profession. She came up with a handful of crumpled greenbacks, a few cents and a tin watch. 'He ain't got no documents nor nuthin'. I guess he's just a dumb butcher. You gonna kill him, Kid?'

'Nah. What I wanna do that fer?' The Kid tossed his grits to hiss in the fire and retrieved his Allen and Hopkins. He slipped it into his holster and examined the butcher's automatic. 'What the hell kinda peashooter's this? I ain't seen one of these afore. How in tarnation you load it?'

'It ain't no good to you, cowboy. You need special clips of bullets. You can't get 'em in these parts.'

'Yeah?' The Kid aimed at a rock and thudded out four slugs. 'Hmm? Not bad.' He shrugged and hurled the weapon out into the night. 'So, it ain't no good to you now.'

'Hey, before you go,' Laverty groaned. 'How about a cup for me?'

'Give him a sup, Della. It was a hard fight.'

'Yeah, you ain't got a bad right yourself for a little 'un. You durn near cracked my ribs. How'm I supposed to drink this?'

'I ain't your nursemaid,' Della said, but held the tin mug to his lips. 'C'mon, git it down.'

'What's a curvy gal like you doin' out here with this no-good varmint?' the butcher asked. 'You oughta be tucked up in bed.'

'Yes,' she grinned, 'and you'd like to be tucking me.'

'Why not? Come on back to Rapid City with me. You ain't in no trouble yet. You choose the Kid's way of life you soon will be.'

The Kid shrugged as he cinched tight the saddle on his pinto. 'He's got a point, Della. You can cut him free in an hour and head back home. I don't need no company.'

'That whorehouse ain't my home. I'm comin' with you, Winnemucca. The more I listen to this guy the more he sounds like some preacher, or teacher, or . . . who knows . . . lawman?'

'Yes.' The half-Sioux put a boot to the bound man's chest, kicking him rolling over. 'So long, snoop.'

Laverty watched the boy and girl leap on to their broncs and head out across the prairie, and, in a while, a verse of the never-ending *Chisholm Trail* drifted back to him in the Kid's clear voice . . . 'Oh, I'll head back south and I'll marry me a squaw, and I'll live all my life on the sunny Washitaw . . . ' And he thought he heard Della's giggle.

'Yeah,' he growled as he put his wrists back to the fire and winced as he tried to burn his bonds.

3

The Black Hills were a geographical anomaly in the heart of what a quarter-century before had been Indian and buffalo country. They rose up as if by magic out of the whispering ocean of the plains, their granite and limestone outcrops silhouetted magnificently against the clear blue sky, their slopes dark with lodgepole pines.

'They look kinda stark but beautiful,' Jed Long whispered with awe as he stepped out from the stage-stop cabin where they had hunkered down overnight. 'You know, Cassie, I think we're gonna be happy here.'

He was a slim young man, in a grey city suit much crumpled now from travelling. With his fingers he scraped his black hair back from his brow, buttoned his once-white shirt, and began to tie his string bow. 'What's the matter, honey?'

Cassie, his bride of two weeks, had a stressed look, unimpressed by the looming scenery. The fresh-faced girl had got little sleep lying on a palliasse on the hard floor of the hovel, listening to the grunts and snores of the other men, the driver, guard, ostler, drummer, and her husband on the other side of the muslin sheet they had politely rigged up. The other young lady, the actress, who had joined the stage at the last outpost of civilization they had passed through, a hick-town on the plains called Etting, had changed into her nightdress to lie beside her. But Cassie had declined to change, staying in her day clothes, afraid of bugs lurking in the palliasse, or the suspiciously smelly blankets provided for them. Now she felt itchy and unwashed, and dreaded another day in the close confinement of the stagecoach, being tossed back and forth like peas in a drum.

'How much longer's it going to take, Jed?' she asked.

'We're nearly there. We should be in Belle Fourche by noon. Then we go on up the trail into the hills to Deadwood. We got a whole new life in front of us, Cass. It's goin' to be great.'

Cassie was not so enthused. Neither of them had ventured west of the Missouri River before. They had been raised in Sioux City, Iowa, and, after their marriage, had set off by steamboat up the Missouri to Fort Pierre, and from there had joined the little bone-crusher stage of the Deadwood City line. As they had left civilization behind them and headed out into a vastness of wilderness Cassie had become more and more homesick. There was a sense inside her of impending misfortune, that they were making a big mistake. 'It's so . . . so wild,' she said. 'I wasn't expecting it to be like this.'

'It's not been much of a honeymoon

so far,' Jed agreed, 'but I'll make it up to you, Cass.'

He watched Cassie wander off to the privy behind the way-station shack, and turned his attentions to their host, a long-bearded recluse, who was aiding the driver to harness fresh horses to the ancient coach. The railroads, the Central Pacific crossing the continent to the south, and the Northern Pacific going from Bismark on the Missouri all the way up to the goldfields of Montana had hit the stage lines hard, but there were still many towns in the great tracts of the American West only accessible by stage, mule and bull-train, or horse-back, and Deadwood was one.

'Your li'l missus ain't used to the hardships of travel,' the wizened ostler hooted. 'I got her a special treat. The hens have laid two eggs. I'll bile up one for her and one for t'other purty gal for their breakfasts.'

'That's kind of you,' Jed Long replied, seeing his wife returning from her ablutions and looking a little fresher. 'You hear that, Cass? You're in luck.'

Cassie nodded brightly. At least it was better than the sow-belly fried in a skillet of grease thickened with flour, with sourdough bread, which was the customary fare provided to travellers on this line.

The actress girl, who had introduced herself as Hetty Pace, was still in her nightdress behind the sheet and pinning up her honey-blonde hair. 'Hi,' she said. 'What's the weather like?'

'Fine,' Cassie replied, making a face. 'Not that it matters when all we have to look forward to is another day being bounced around in that bucket.'

'Well, at least it's summer and all we have is the dust to contend with. They say in winter it's advisable to get out to walk up every hill to stop your feet from freezing off. The men spend most the time hauling the coach out of sage bogs.'

'That's something, I s'pose,' Cassie agreed. 'It's just that as we're on the verge of the twentieth century I've gotten used to home comforts. I guess I wasn't expecting this country to still be so desolate, so primitive.'

'Look on the bright side, Cassie. At least we won't have Red Cloud and his painted savages coming riding out of the blue howling for our scalps. They're mostly on the reservations now.'

'I don't know how you can be so cheerful.' Cassie watched the lissom young actress dressing in her long-skirted dove-grey costume and buttoning her bootees. 'I guess you're used to travelling?'

'Us theatricals get used to anything. We're always on the move.' Hetty gave her a wide smile as she pinned on a rather preposterous hat. 'Our life isn't as glamorous as people imagine. Where's that boiled egg and coffee I've been hearing about?'

They made a hurried breakfast as the driver was shouting that they were ready to go. He was throwing their bags into the canvas carrier at the rear, and gathering the reins in his hands. 'All aboard, folks. Belle Fourche next stop.'

They hurriedly climbed into the ramshackle Concord to sit in close confinement, Cassie and Jed on one side, Hetty seated opposite, next to the flabby-jowled drummer, or travelling salesman, outfitted in vulgar colours, a check suit, spats, and top hat. 'Oh, my Lord,' he trilled, hanging on as they set off. 'Here we go again.'

The coach creaked, jolted, swayed, crawled up hill, made reckless dashes downwards, crossed streams, and performed all kinds of stunts except turning over, jolting the passengers back and forth as they followed the Belle Fourche River and climbed towards the Black Hills.

The drummer constantly mopped at his perspiring brow and neck and took a silver flask from his pocket to take discreet nips. It was indeed hot, a stultifying heat indicative of an approaching storm. The canvas shutters had been rolled down to try to keep out the fine powdery dust raised by the horses' twelve pairs of hooves, but this only made it hotter still.

Cassie sighed and touched fingers to her brow. 'I've such a headache,' she said.

'I've just the thing for you.' The salesman eagerly opened his carpet bag, and produced a small bottle. 'Aspirin it's called. Really works wonders. Dried myrtle leaves and willow bark are the active ingredients, salicylic acid. Tried and tested. Only put on the market in January this year, but already people are raving about it.'

'Oh, yeah,' Jed smiled. 'That's what you are, eh? A snakeoil salesman.'

'No, this is from Germany, the Bayer company, so it must be good. And, look, it's in pill form. Not the usual powder. Try a couple, my dear. And if in an hour your headache hasn't gone I'll eat my hat. That will be one dollar for the bottle, dear sir.'

'Yeah?' Jed dug out a dollar. 'Maybe it's worth a try.'

'Would you have anything for a sore throat?' Hetty asked. 'All the singing I do, I've really gone quite hoarse.'

'Indeed, yes, sweetheart.' The drummer produced another small bottle, labelled 'Heroin,' and passed it across. 'It's related to morphine. We are promoting it as the perfect cough remedy.'

Hetty studied the label quizzically as the stage rolled back and forth. 'I'm not sure about these quack medicines.' She handed it back. 'I think I'll stick to a spoonful of honey in my tea.'

'Please yourself.' The drummer's look of prim annoyance at a lost sale turned to one of anxiety as he heard the driver shouting out, 'Whoa-down-thuh,' and hauling the stage to a halt. 'What's this varmint want?'

Jed stuck his head out of the coach and saw a burly man in a suit and derby hat standing by the trail. 'Looks like some fellow wants to get on board.'

The guard was pointing his shotgun and growling, 'Keep your hands high and come along here.' The man did so. He did not appear to be armed. At least, he had no ammunition belt or gun on his hip.

'I've been robbed,' the butcher said. 'Two of 'em. They buffaloed me, took my horse. Look at this egg on the back of my head.'

'You better git inside,' the driver shouted.

'There's no room in here,' the drummer protested.

Bill Lawson, alias Laverty, jerked open the door. 'There would be,' he grinned, 'if you got up on top.'

The drummer squawked as the big man pushed inside and squeezed between him and the actress. 'Really, the manners of a warthog.'

The driver cracked the whip and they were on their way again. The 'butcher' tipped his hat to the ladies.

'Never thought I'd be travelling in such fragrant company,' he smiled. 'Where you heading, sir?'

'My wife and I are travelling to

Deadwood. We plan to open our own store. My maiden aunt died and bequested it to me.'

'Really?' The older man's stout chest and biceps were almost bursting from a dusty grey four-button suit and vest. His pugnacious nose and rocky jaw gave him the look of a prize-fighter as he took off his curly-brimmed hat. 'You in that line of business?'

'Well, yes,' Jed replied. 'Cassie and I were both store clerks. In the same store in Sioux City. That's where we met. Then, as I say, my Aunt Hannah died and I decided it was too good an opportunity to miss — to be my own boss. I understand it's a restaurant of sorts. Would you know it? It's number forty-four Deadwood Gulch.'

'Number forty-four?' The pug-faced man grinned his surprise. 'Saloon forty-four you mean. Hannah's joint. Hard-hearted Hannah. No disrespect to your aunt's memory, mister. She might have been unmarried but I hardly think she was a maid. That's one of the rowdiest bawdy-houses in town.'

'What?' Cassie screeched, her jaw dropping with astonishment. 'What's he mean, Jed?'

'Nothing, dear.' He frowned at Lawson and shook his head. 'Whatever it *might* have been *our's* will be a respectable business.'

'That's funny,' Hetty smiled. 'Number forty-four is on my itinerary. I'm due for a three-night stand after a two-nighter at Belle Fourche.'

'You don't say,' Lawson grinned. 'I'd be glad of a one-night stand with you any time.'

A blush prickled into Hetty's cheeks. 'You misunderstand me, sir. I am a travelling singer on a tour of the West arranged by my agent. I had no idea number forty-four Deadwood Gulch was an establishment of ill-repute. Really, how scandalous.'

'I beg your pardon, miss. You're obviously not that kind of entertainer. Although, you can't go by appearances these days. You're a damned good-looker and some of those gals dress like you in the height of fashion.'

'Watch your language,' Jed warned. 'You're being very rude, mister.'

'Yes, very uncouth,' the drummer remarked, and gave a squawk as the coach rolled and he was hurled against Lawson.

The butcher gave a heave of his shoulders and threw him back into his corner. 'I was only joking,' he growled.

'That's OK,' Hetty smiled, 'I can assure you I'm highly respectable. But I'm pestered by stage-door Johnnies all the time. If I took offence at every fool remark — '

'So, what's Deadwood like?' Jed asked. 'It's surely not as rough and ready a mining town as in the old days?'

'No, they've got a vigilante force of sixty men so it's pretty law-abiding these days.' Lawson's little grey eyes glimmered with amusement so they weren't sure whether he was bluffing or telling the truth. 'But you could say the main cause of death is still liquor or lead.'

'I'd appreciate it if you'd change the tone of this conversation,' Jed said, hugging Cassie to him. 'You're upsetting my wife.'

'He's teasing us,' Hetty put in.

'Sure I am.' Lawson gave her a wink as he pulled out a cheroot. 'You ladies mind if I smoke?'

'If you are determined to be offensive,' Hetty replied, 'I suggest you ride on top. Mrs Long is already feeling sick.'

'I know when I'm not wanted.' Lawson lit up, rammed on his derby at a jaunty angle, and opened the door. 'I'll git some fresh air. So long, folks.' He clambered out and swung up to a seat behind the box.

'Odd fellow,' Jed said, as he pulled the door shut. 'Abrupt manner, but I couldn't help liking him, in a way.'

'Did you see he was wearing a shoulder holster under his suit,' the drummer squeaked. 'I think he's a dangerous character. We ought to inform the law enforcement officer when we get to Belle Fourche.'

'Oh, I think he's all right,' Hetty sighed, but glad not to be so closely squashed. 'Most men carry a gun in these parts.'

'Yes,' Jed muttered. 'Perhaps I should think of getting myself one.'

4

The Winnemucca Kid had made good time, riding the butcher's bay to give his pinto a rest, Della trotting alongside on her sturdy pony. They reached the Belle Fourche River and followed it west towards the great Wyoming plain where, only twenty-five years before, 20,000 Sioux and Cheyenne warriors had fought a bitter battle to defend their last domain. After the Custer massacre in '76 the tribes had put up a scattered resistance, but they were either blown to atoms by the army's howitzers, or deported to bleak reservations. Where there had once been millions of buffalo grazing this green ocean, there were now herds of cattle. And with cattle came — wire!

'Hell take them!' Winnemucca cursed as their path was blocked by a fence. 'I hate this stuff.' He jumped from the

41

bay, took a pair of wire-cutters from his saddle-bag and attacked it. The wire sprang coiling back, its barbs digging into his arm. 'Yow!' He sucked at the bloody tear and swore some more as he disentangled himself and cut away the fence. 'I hate being fenced in. And I hate these dang white folk who think they can come and fence off our open range.'

'They ain't gonna like you cutting down their wire, Kid.'

'Hell take 'em.' He sprang back on the pinto. 'Let's go.'

They camped out that night in a creek of cotton-woods and wild roses as a scattering of pinkly-flushed cumulus clouds were blown away across the great Wyoming sky. As night set in they sat beside their fire and cooked the haunch of a small antelope the Kid had shot. As they did so wolves skulked up to watch them, their eyes glittering in the firelight's reflection, almost as if they wanted to join them by the fireside.

'It's lonesome out here, ain't it?' Della said, as she snuggled up beside him. 'You say you hate white folks, but you're half-white yourself, ain't that so?'

'Yep.' He tossed a stick into the flames. 'My mammy was a white gal crossing the plains in a wagon train when a war party of Sioux struck. They were led by a warrior called Two Horns on account of the buffalo mask he wore. He raped her and slaughtered most of the rest. It musta happened somewhere around here. She survived and got back to Fort Laramie. She joined a party of Mormons who were heading out to Utah and Nevada and nine months later I was born. But my mammy musta taken one look at me and decided she didn't want nuthin' to do with no half-breed. She left me to be brought up by a Mormon couple in the little town of Winnemucca, and headed back East.'

'So, didn't you ever see or hear from her again?'

'Nope.' A touch of bitterness hardened his dark face. 'That was twenty-two summers ago. Those Mormons brought me up like one of their'n. Mormons have always given the hand of friendship to Indians. They're good people. But all that churchifying and gospel singing kinda got me down. An' all that they kept drummin' into me 'bout you mustn't drink whiskey, or smoke, or go with bad girls, it just made me want to try them things the more. I lit out seven years ago and I ain't looked back. I guess you could say the devil tempted me.'

'Me too, Kid. I ran off from home when I was fifteen. I guess we're two of a kind.'

'Don't get no ideas. I'm me.' He touched his chest proudly. 'I'm on my own. I ain't nuthin' to do with you. And I ain't planning on gittin' hitched to no whore. It ain't right. Gals didn't ought to be like you.'

'Wow! Them Mormons certainly turned you into a mealy-mouthed puritan underneath. But, I guess you're right,' she sighed. 'I ain't happy about doing them things, but what else can a gal do?'

When he didn't reply she shrugged and asked, 'Didn't you ever want to find out what happened to your mother?'

'Nope. If she didn't want me, why should I want her? Anyhow, where the hell would I start? All I got left of her is half a broken piece of wood, see?' He fished out a piece of petrified wood struck by lightning on a cord of buckskin around his bronzed throat. 'It seems she tore this from my father's throat when he attacked her and for some reason hung on to it. It must have been his power 'cause he was shot by the army soon after.'

Della fingered it, curiously. 'Who's got the other half?'

'She has. Apparently she told them Mormons that she would hang on to the other half and if we ever met again that's how she would know me. I've hung on to it since I was a kid. I don't know why. I must be crazy. I ain't never goin' to see her again. But I guess I must be superstitious. I kinda regard it as my own power. It's all I got left of my family.'

He swallowed his emotion as he tucked the amulet back in his shirt, and lay and stared into the fire for some while, his thoughts drifting back into the past, wondering about her. What she looked like, wondering why she had abandoned him.

To change the subject Della asked, 'Where we goin', Kid?'

'To the Hole-in-the-Wall. It's a hideout of a gang led by a pal of mine. We met in Jackson jail. I was doing six months for appropriating a few cattle didn't belong to me. He's a wild ugly bastard called Dan Hogan. That jail didn't hold him long. He broke out and left a note saying he'd gone to see his sick granny.'

'So, where is this Hole?'

'Up in the Big Horn mountains.'

Della smiled and slipped her fingers into the studs of his jeans. 'There's only one Big Horn I'm interested in.'

'Yeah?' He fondled her hair and flashed her a grin in the firelight. 'You don't say.'

★　★　★

'Wake up, Della,' the Kid whispered. 'We got company.'

The rising sun was flashing across the plain to bathe great stacks of clouds in pink and crimson. And from beneath this seething mountain of approaching storm were riding five darkly silhouetted men. The Kid kneeled in the damp grass and levelled his Winchester.

'Well, I'll be damned,' he drawled. 'It's Dan Hogan.'

He could hardly fail to recognize the leading horseman, a grotesque, stumpy-legged man, his gargantuan head, covered in greasy black hair, out of all proportion to his body. When the Kid showed himself, Hogan whirled his mustang and snatched his own carbine from the saddle boot.

'It's me!' The Kid waved his Winchester over his head, and Hogan came spurring towards him.

'Winnemucca, you young varmint. What kept you?' The Gorgon, as some called him behind his back, sprang from his saddle and wrapped long apelike arms around the Kid, pressing him to his barrel chest, and tossing him in the air as if he were no more than a babe in arms. 'This is the Kid I tole ya 'bout,' he roared. 'We did time in Jackson jail.'

The two men started mock-punching the dust out of each other's clothes. 'Yeah,' the Kid grinned. 'They tightened up security after you lit out, put a leg-iron on me.'

'Sorry I couldn't take you along. I was in a bit of a hurry.' Hogan's swarthy features were dominated by wide nostrils and black bulging eyes which suddenly lighted on Della. 'Who's she?'

'Della Rose. She used to work on her

back, but now she figures she's gonna be an outlaw like me.'

Hogan extended his massive paw to grip her hand. 'Well, I nevuh! You got yourself a gal.'

He gave a hoot of glee and doffed his fist at a younger version of himself, not quite so broad, or as ugly, but ugly enough in nature. 'This is my kid brother, Donny.'

Donny nodded, surlily unsmiling, and fingered his carbine.

'There's Polly.' Hogan fingered an old man with a birdlike beak, who touched his hatbrim. 'George Parrott. He boasts he can open a safe quicker than a whore can drop her drawers.

'This here's Joe Pizanthia.' A slim Latino-'Texican', his father Texan and his mother Mexican, stroked his moustachios, and removed his sombrero with exaggerated courtesy.

'An' that's Ten-Spot Jones.' A straw-haired, lanky cowboy grinned, goofily.

'So, where you goin', Dan?'

'To bust the bank in Belle Fourche. I

got inside information there's twenty thousand smackeroos in the safe there. Wanna come along?'

'Sure, where's the rest of your gang?'

'I left 'em to guard the Hole. What about the gal?'

'I can ride and shoot good as anyone,' Della scoffed. 'I ain't jest come along to cook an' wash your socks, or whatever. I aim to be a regular outlaw.'

'So, let's ride.'

The Kid and Della turned back with them along the meandering river. The girl glanced at the scruffily-dressed men as they cantered along. They were a hard bunch, an edge of danger about them, ready for anything, and God help anybody who got in the way. It was good to be out in the open air away from the sleazy saloons. An excitement pumped through her, mingled with awe. Jeez, she thought, what have I got myself into this time?

'Looks like a storm blowing up,' Donny shouted, turning in the saddle to look back at dark viridian clouds billowing up above the prairie behind them. There was an urgent rumble of thunder, and flicker of lightning. 'Ain't it best to git off the broncs, Dan?'

The reason he said so was the amount of iron they were carrying, rifles and carbines in the saddle holsters, the mustangs' bits, their shoes. They made fine conductors of electricity. Some cowboys were prone to pull off their spurs, throw aside their revolver and ammunition belt, and hunker down in the open until such storms had passed.

'Aw, what's a l'il storm?' Hogan spurred his horse on with rugged fatalism. 'If we git hit, we git hit. We'll be fryin' in hell soon enough.'

The others charged on after him, their mounts laying back their ears in fear as the air about them turned black, a clap of thunder resounded like ten thousand war drums, and shafts of forked lightning scorched the ground about them. A scent like brimstone reeked in their nostrils, and a blinding bolt split a cottonwood not fifty feet away as they galloped by. For moments it was as if the gods meant to strike them down as more lashes of lightning almost singed their eyebrows. And then the atmosphere turned brittle cold and hailstones the size of eggs rattled down like buckshot.

But soon the storm had passed and they were back under blue skies. Hogan grinned at them, 'I tell ya, Della, I live a charmed life. You stick with me you'll be all right.'

They hit the main trail from Miles City in the north and cantered south along it, pulling their mounts into a halt outside the town saloon in Belle Fourche. They loose-hitched their mustangs by the water butt, climbed on to the raised sidewalk, and clattered into the bar. Della would have preferred a cup of coffee, but joined the boys in splitting a bottle of red-eye. She had to act tough. They stood by the window and peered across the dirt street to the bank. It was the only brick building in the street.

'You sure about this?' Hogan growled, getting on a chair to peer over the curtain. 'The information, I mean.'

'Sure I'm sure.' Pizanthia's eyes glimmered beneath the wide brim of his sombrero. 'We go for it, huh?'

5

'Here comes the stage,' Dan Hogan said, as the Fort Pierre to Deadwood City coach came rolling in. 'We better wait awhile.'

The stagecoach stopped at the Wells Fargo office along from the bank. A small crowd of bystanders was milling about to see if there was any mail for them. A portly drummer tumbled out. A broad-shouldered gent in a derby hat jumped down and offered his hand to an attractive blonde lady in a large hat. And a slimly handsome young couple also stepped out.

Up on his box the driver pointed his whip at another waiting coach and hollered, 'Connection for Miles City about to pull out. You other folks can stretch your legs and git some grub 'fore we move off for Deadwood.' He started the horses away along to the livery to harness a fresh team.

The passengers sauntered over towards a restaurant. 'I'm gonna buy me a carbine,' Bill Lawson told them. 'I'll join you in a minute.' Although robbed, he had ten golden 'twenties' secreted in his boot-heels.

When the Miles City coach set off, kicking up a cloud of dust, most of the onlookers drifted away, too. Hogan muttered, 'OK, let's go. Della, you hang on to the hosses, and have 'em ready when we come out.'

Dan Hogan led the way across the street, holding a carpet bag. Della could not help smiling, he looked so comical, his big butt waggling as he walked, his four-feet-six size diminutive against the lofty Pizanthia in his tall hat and the lanky Ten Spot on either side of him. Donny, the Kid, and George Parrot hurried behind them. She climbed on to her own bronc and gathered the reins of the other six horses, no easy task.

Hogan entered the bank, strutted up

to the cashier's grille and peered over the counter. 'I wanna make a withdrawal.'

'Have you an account with us, sir?'

'No. I just wanta make a withdrawal. Here.' Hogan shoved his bag through the hole. 'Fill it up outa the safe. I want everything you got.'

'Is this your idea of a joke, sir?' The cashier jerked his polished shoe under a wire beneath his desk and looked across at another teller. 'I'm afraid we can't help you.'

'Fill it up, I said.' Dan Hogan jerked a heavy Remington revolver out of his coat pocket and poked it through the hole. 'Or else. No, I sure ain't joking.'

There were a couple of other customers waiting to carry out transactions, a farmer's wife, and a man dressed like an undertaker in Lincoln hat and black frock coat. They looked around, startled, as Donny, the Kid and Parrot pushed into the bank, brandishing carbines.

'Having trouble?' Donny called.

'No, I'm trying to explain to this little shithead that this is a hold-up. He don't seem to get it.'

'Blow his damn head off, Dan.'

The clerk's voice quavered as he peered through at them. 'I'm sorry, sir, I still can't help you. You see, it's Saturday, early closing, and the manager's just caught the stage to Miles City. He won't be back until Monday. There's no way we can open it. The safe's on a time lock.'

Hogan's jaw dropped and his brother hissed, 'I told ya we shoulda brought some dynamite.'

'Polly, get round there, see what you can do. Open up this gate, mister. If you're lying I wouldn't want to be in your shoes.'

The clerk produced his keys to open up and let them through. His eyes bulged as Hogan jabbed his Remington under his jaw. 'I'm afraid it's so, sir. The manager don't seem to trust me. Try to open the safe yourself. There's no way.'

Hogan waggled at the safe handle. It

was true. It would not give. 'Try it, Polly. You're supposed to be the expert.'

Parrot Nose blew on his fingers, wiggled them, and began tampering with the combination lock, tapping it with his revolver butt, listening. 'That's strange. Won't open. Must be one of them special Yale locks.'

'How much *have* you got in here?' Hogan demanded.

'About fifteen thousand dollars, sir.'

'Shee-it! What you got in the drawer? Open it.' He started picking out the cash. 'Seventy dollars, seventy cents,' he groaned. 'Hell, we come all this way for this?'

'We shoulda struck,' Donny yelled, angrily, ''fore the damn manager caught the stage.'

'How was I to know?' Hogan bellowed.

Suddenly the outlaws froze as they heard a loud voice outside. 'All right, you in there. Throw your weapons out and come out with your hands up. You ain't got a chance. You're surrounded.'

'Come on,' Hogan growled, his heart sinking. 'I ain't going back to no penitentiary.'

The men looked at each other as the undertaker wheedled, 'The wisest thing would be to surrender, boys. That's the sheriff out there.'

Hogan gripped his Remingon and nodded grimly at his brother. 'Don't you worry, mister, there may be some business come your way. Git your tape measure ready.'

'Hey, you weasel!' Donny scowled at the chief clerk as he saw the telltale wire leading away through a hole in the wall, no doubt connecting with a bell in the sheriff's office. 'It was you tipped them off.'

'I'm sorry,' the teller stuttered. 'My foot slipped.'

Dan Hogan clouted him across the jaw with his Remington, felling him. 'Come on, boys,' he shouted, wildly, leading them towards the door. 'Let's go for it.'

Hogan, Donny, Mexican Joe, Parrot

Nose George, the Kid and Ten Spot poured out of the bank at a run, revolvers and carbines blazing. Men ranged on the sidewalk opposite pumped a fusillade of bullets stuttering into the bank's brick walls. Polly Parrot caught lead in the chest and went spinning from the sidewalk into the street, blood pouring from him. Joe was hit in the thigh and went sprawling, too. But the others were luckier, running at a crouch out along the sidewalk, ducking down behind barrels, wagons and horses, wildly returning fire.

'Here comes Della,' Donny shouted.

The girl, dragging her string of mustangs, who were snorting, kicking and eye-rolling their fear, came at a canter along the street braving the flying lead. The outlaws, those still standing, ran to snatch hold of bridles and swing into saddles as the horses raced by. And they were away, yelling and whooping, crashing out shots at anyone who showed themselves with guns in hands.

'What in tarnation's goin' on?' Bill Lawson jumped up from the table in the restaurant and ran to the open door, his new-bought Springfield already at his shoulder. He knelt and aimed at one of the riders and sent Ten Spot catapulting from his saddle to lie dead and bleeding in the road.

Dan Hogan had pulled a carbine from his saddle boot. He gave a roar of anger and turned it on whoever it was firing from the restaurant door. Inside, the drummer screamed, Hetty ducked for cover, but Jed Long was standing up, drawing Cassie to one side for safety when Hogan's bullet smashed through the window. Cassie cried out and went limp in his arms. He lay her on the floor and it was as if his heart had gone icy cold with shock and fear.

Donny was galloping after his brother and he too let loose a couple of slugs from his revolver at the marksman in the café doorway, who had downed Ten Spot. He got lucky, but not so Lawson, who dropped the Springfield as lead tore like fire into his left shoulder. He gasped and watched the gunmen go thundering out of town as bullets zipped like angry bees about their heads.

'Why?' Cassie pleaded as she stared up at Jed, cradled in his arms. 'Why us?'

'Hang on, Cass. You're going to be all right.' But he could see a large patch of scarlet blood flowering through the blouse high on her chest. And the light in her eyes suddenly faded. 'No, Cass,' he sobbed. 'Oh, God, no.'

Lawson looked back and saw the young fellow, tears streaming from his eyes, hugging the dead girl. 'Aw, hell,' he growled.

★ ★ ★

The robbers rode at a headlong gallop following the narrow winding trail up into the Black Hills towards Deadwood until they hauled in to take stock of their situation and suddenly heard hoofbeats.

'It's Joe.'

The Tex-Mex had managed to reach a horse, and somehow drag himself on board, but his thigh was bleeding profusely. 'They got Polly and Ten Spot,' he cried. 'They're both dead.'

'Yeah, too bad,' Hogan grunted. 'Come on, we gotta beat it.'

'Wait a minute,' Della said, jumping down to look at the bloody hole in Joe Pizanthia's thigh. She whipped off her bandanna and began to tie it tight. 'That should hold it a bit.'

'If he cain't keep up, we ain't waiting,' Donny shouted, putting spurs to his bronc and setting off on up the trail.

Dan Hogan shrugged and hauled his mustang around, and led them chasing after him. After another mile or so they reined in, their horses blowing hard. There was an eerie silence about them in the pine forest. They listened intently, and suddenly heard the drum-beat of hooves coming at a gallop up the trail. 'Aw, shee-it,' Hogan groaned.

'They comin' arter us. What fer, seventy friggin' dollars?'

Donny pointed up a canyon and yelled, 'I think there's a way up through here we kin get round the back of Deadwood and through the hills.'

'Some way out,' Hogan snarled as they reached the end of the steep box canyon and were faced by a sheer precipice.

'Maybe they gone straight on past,' Donny ventured.

'Maybe they ain't,' Hogan growled, as he glimpsed men climbing up through the pines towards them. 'We gonna have to hold out here. It ain't Friday the thirteenth, by any chance? We ain't having much luck.'

Hogan levered a slug into his carbine as the others took cover behind rocks and Della hurriedly led the horses to one side. 'Make every bullet count, boys. We ain't got unlimited ammunition.'

The Belle Fourche sheriff and his ten men had the robbers cornered up in the rocks. With righteous anger they blazed away, but were cautious, too, none willing to make a charge at those on the higher ground. Bullets blammed, whined and ricocheted back and forth chipping rocks, but pretty soon the battle became a stalemate.

'Hold your fire,' Hogan muttered, taking off his greasy Stetson and mopping at his brow as the late afternoon sun beat down on his back. 'It ain't long to sundown. We'll make a break for it when it gets dark.'

'Joe don't look too good,' the Kid said.

Della turned her attention to Pizanthia, who, indeed, looked in a bad way. She tried washing the wound with water from a canteen before plugging the hole in the thigh with his own bandanna. 'Maybe I can tie mine tight like a tourniquet, slow the bleeding down,' she whispered. 'How's that, Joe?'

'Ees OK,' he said, giving a grimace of pain.

'Don't waste the water on that

greaser,' Donny shouted. 'We ain't got much.' He snatched the wooden canteen away and put it to his mouth.

'Don't you waste it neither,' Hogan said, snatching it from his brother. 'Give it to the hosses, Della. They need it more than us. They gotta git us outa here.'

Sporadic firing continued from both sides until the sun slipped away over the crest of the precipice, shadows lengthened and darkness fell.

'Look, they've lit a fire. They're cooking 'emselves supper,' Hogan said, peering down at shadowy shapes around a camp-fire among the trees. 'They must think they're setting in for a siege. Now's our chance for a break. Hit 'em with everything we got.'

Della helped the Kid put Joe on to his horse and watched, anxiously, as he put the reins in his teeth, straightened his sombrero, and levered his carbine, snapping a slug into the breech. The Hogan brothers climbed on to their own mustangs, cocking their revolvers.

She and the Kid followed suit.

'Ready?' Dan Hogan asked. 'Let's go.'

They sent their broncs charging and ploughing down through the talus towards the trees. There was a warning cry and a flash of gunshot. But they were already upon them, firing at the men around the campfire, leaping their horses through them, shooting point blank at shadowy figures, scattering them, and swerving and weaving on down through the pines until they hit the trail.

'Which way?' Donny shouted.

'Up through to Deadwood,' Dan Hogan replied.

But he had made the wrong decision. On a bend of the trail the fugitives ran slap bang into forty riders of the Deadwood vigilance committee, summoned to help the Belle Fourche posse. They were surrounded and could do nothing but surrender their arms.

'Shall we string 'em up now?' one of the riders asked. 'What say you, Sheriff

Wyler? It would save you some paperwork.'

'No, I gotta act according to the law,' the Deadwood lawman drawled. 'We'll give 'em a fair trial in the mornin' and hold the hanging at four in the afternoon. Folks like to see justice bein' done.'

'They sure are an ugly lookin' bunch,' one of the others said, striking a match and peering up close in the darkness. 'Hey, this one looks like a gal.' He leaned over and groped at her breasts under her coat. 'Hey, she is, too.'

'Keep your hands to yourself, you dirty old bastard,' Della growled, as others laughed and jostled about her to try to get a look.

6

'Get in there, Hogan. We been waiting a long time to get you.' Sheriff John Wyler thrust Dan Hogan into his office at Deadwood. 'Empty your pockets. You'll be kicking the clouds tomorrow.'

'What for? I'm innocent. I ain't killed nobody.'

'No? What about a young woman, Mrs Cassie Long, you shot as you made your escape? The poor gal had only been married two weeks.'

'What gal? I didn't shoot no female. I ain't the sort to do that.'

'You may not have intended to but you surely did, and you'll have to pay. You, too,' the sheriff said, looking at the Kid, Donny, Della and Pizanthia, who was pushed limping in. 'You were all involved together, so you're all for the big jump, believe me.'

'Della didn't kill nobody,' Pizanthia

gasped out. 'She just hold the horses.'

'Della, is it? Well, if you're so fond of her you can share a cell. And you,' the sheriff said, shoving Donny up against the wall. 'By the look of your criminal configurations you must be the ugly little brother. I got a Wanted poster on you, too.'

Hogan suddenly exploded with rage, picking up the desk and hurling it at the sheriff, pinning him against the wall. 'You — ' He screamed obscenities at Wyler as the deputies tried to pull him off.

One of the legs of the desk was already broken, attached to the stump by a length of wire. Hogan tore the loose leg away, turning to belabour the men with this club. His brother, Donny, joined in the affray, and the men had their hands full trying to overpower the frenzied Hogans. Donny was even crazier than his older brother, if that were possible, and was flailing and kicking, gone berserk. Hogan grinned as he lay on the floor between the stomping legs and watched. He quickly picked up the piece of wire and stuffed it in his pocket. Who knew, it might come in useful!

When order was restored and the deputies had kicked the stuffing out of both Hogans they were thrown into a cell opposite one containing the Kid, Della, Joe and an old drunk called Dan Dafoe.

Sheriff Wyler looked at the mess made of his office, the broken chair and desk, papers strewn all over the place. 'OK, boys,' he drawled to his deputies and the vigilance men. 'These varmints are all locked up for the night. They won't give us no more trouble. I'll tidy up here. You can go over the saloon, drinks on me. You've earned it.'

Della looked across at the squat, hairy Hogan who was glowering through the bars of his cell, wiping blood from his nose. 'You sure got a hate on for lawmen, aincha Dan?'

'Thass the truth, Della. You better believe it. Well, a fine mess I got us all into.' He shook his shaggy head. 'Some gal dead, huh? I hate to hear that.'

'Aw, you win some, you lose some,' Donny said. 'How was you to know?'

The Kid gripped the bars of the cell, testing them. 'We certainly ain't gonna git outa here.'

'That's for certain,' Sheriff Wyler called from his office around the corner, as the men trooped out and he closed the door on them. 'Look at this damn desk. It's finished now.' They heard a rattling and scraping as he pitched it out into the street. 'All it's worth is firewood. Hogan,' he shouted, 'I'm gonna make doubly sure you hang for this.'

'How about some food?' Donny called back. 'Prisoners got rights, you know.'

'Sonny, you can starve to death for all I care.'

They heard him grunting and muttering as he straightened his papers and tidied up. Dan Hogan looked across at Della and hissed, 'Call him along and keep him talking. I got an idea.'

The bearded, booze-stinking Dan Dafoe had come out of his stupor and was beaming at Della, stroking her leg. 'Are you a gal, missy, under them clothes? Shucks, ain't that kind of the sheriff. We're gonna have some fun.'

'Sheriff!' Della screeched. 'There's a drunk in my cell molesting me. This ain't right. It ain't decent. Get this scumbag outa here.'

'Too bad,' Wyler called, from around his corner. 'You'll have to lump it. We ain't got no other accommodations. And you sure ain't as pure as the driven snow.'

'This Mex here's in a bad way. He needs a medic to get the bullet outa his leg.'

'He'll survive. If not, too bad. He'll miss his hanging. So shuddup.'

Della shrugged at Hogan, who hissed, 'Try again.'

'Sheriff!' she screamed. 'I got a confession to make.'

Wyler, a star pinned to his denim

shirt, his gunbelt hitched over one hip, ambled along to them, taking a stance in the centre of the wide corridor, keeping a good distance from either side. He glanced at the Hogans who were sat down on their bunks. And, hands on his hips, he turned to meet Della's eyes. 'So, what is it you want to confess?'

'I've been a bad girl. I shoulda stayed in Rapid City. I should never have come with them. Sheriff, if I tell you what I know, will you give me a break?'

'Maybe. That depends. The judge might take into account your gender, your age. Nobody likes to hang a gal. Come on, spit it out. What you got to say?'

'Well, you remember that bank robbery in Denver back in ninety-seven, two years ago? They got away with five thousand dollars?'

'Yeah, what about it?'

'They told me that they did that.'

'Who — ?' If her words came as a surprise to the sheriff, the wire noose tossed by Hogan's long apelike arms to drop neatly over his head came, by the expression on his face, as even more of one. 'Aagh,' he croaked, as the wire was jerked back and he was dragged tight to the bars. The sheriff flailed to get at his Colt .45, but Donny Logan was there first, his hand poking through and whipping it from the holster.

The sheriff's gasped groan became incomprehensible as the wire tightened, biting into his throat. Donny was unbuckling his belt, taking the keys from it, but there was nothing Wyler could do. His eyes bulged as the wire cut off his breath.

Hogan braced his muscles and tightened the noose, listening to the death croak. 'Hang me, would you? Huh, the cheek of the guy.'

Those in the opposite cell watched with fascinated horror as Wyler slid to the floor, and there was silence for seconds before Della breathed out, 'Jeez, Dan, you didn't need to kill the guy.'

'Yeah.' The Kid looked sick. 'That weren't wise.'

'Hurry it up, Donny.' Hogan watched his brother manoeuvre the keys into the lock before he found the right one. 'Those guys might be back any minute.'

Donny turned a key and the cell door swung open.

'What's the matter, Della?' Hogan sneered. 'Maybe I should leave you and the Kid there? Maybe you don't want to come along? Why you both talkin' like damn Sunday school teachers?'

He kneeled down and went through Wyler's pockets, pulling out a roll of dollars. 'This must be what he took off us.'

'Hey,' Donny shouted from the office. 'All our guns are here.'

'Good. All we need now is to find our broncs, or fresh ones.' Hogan hopped about pulling his boots back on. 'Della don't want to join us. We're too damn low for her taste.'

'Yeah, an' she was mighty quick to

start blabbing about that Denver job, eh, Dan?'

'I was trying to distract him, you durn idjit. I couldn't think what else to say.'

'C'mon, Donny, let's go.'

'Aw, c'mon, boys,' the Kid wheedled. 'Don't leave us here.' But the door slammed. He turned to the others. 'Holy Mother, would you believe it?'

'I ain't the Holy Mother,' Dan Dafoe wheezed.

A few seconds later the jailhouse door opened and Hogan stuck his grinning gargoyle head through. 'Heh! Heh! Fooled you! Serve you durn right.' He stomped back to unlock their cell. 'They left the hosses round the back.'

Della raised her eyes heavenwards as she helped Pizanthia hop out. 'These guys!' She slammed the door shut on Dan and locked it. 'Not you, grandad. Go back to sleep.'

Pizanthia shook his head and made the sign of the cross as he looked down at the body of Wyler. 'Those two, they are real cold-blooded killers. There was no need to do that.'

'Yes,' Della said. 'They give me the creeps, too. Come on, Joe, we gotta ride. We gotta get outa here 'fore they string us all high.'

7

'Ashes to ashes and dust to dust,' the preacher intoned, making the sign of the cross over the pine coffin of Cassie Long as she was lowered into her grave. 'We bring nuthin' into this world, and, to be sure, we take nuthin' out. The Lord giveth and the Lord taketh away.'

Jed stared at the box. He was standing between Bill Lawson and Hetty Pace, serious of face in her large flowered hat. A scattering of sympathizers had followed the hearse out to a small graveyard set beneath gloomy pines on a bend of the river.

'Friends, let us pray for the departed and join together in one of the good old hymns of long ago, 'Sweet By And By',' the preacher called. 'To be followed by 'On the Other Side of Jordan'.'

The congregation joined lustily in the hymns, but the strong river breeze whipped the words from their mouths. One by one they stooped to throw a handful of dirt onto the coffin. Jed stood frozen and horrified as it was lowered into the hole and a man with a spade stepped forward.

'Why?' Jed Long shouted, in a choking voice. 'Why us? What have we done to deserve this? She was a sweet, innocent girl. She never hurt anyone. Why should the Lord take her away?'

'He has His reasons we cannot fathom.' The preacher looked like a gaunt crow, his black frock coat flapping in the wind. 'He has called her to His shining kingdom,' he said, as they began to fill in the grave. 'She will find a greater happiness there than on this earth.'

'Somebody's got to pay,' Jed gritted out.

'Steady,' Bill Lawson murmured, gripping his arm, for the distraught young Long looked about ready to fall on the grave. 'She's gone, boy. You gotta face that fact.'

The few folks about the grave began to sing, 'We shall gather by the river . . . the beautiful, the beautiful, river . . . '

And the Belle Fourche stream nearby sparkled in the summer sunshine, its waters sweeping by. All that was left of Cassie was a rugged wooden cross and a memory.

Jed kneeled for a long while by the grave after the preacher and mourners had trailed away on their horses and buggies. 'I'm not going to forgive.' He turned his tear-stained face up to Hetty and Lawson. 'I'm not going to forget. I want vengeance. I'm going to track them down and bring them back for hanging, all those who did this to my girl. I vow that now. God be my witness.'

Lawson had his arm in a sling from the shoulder wound he had sustained. But the quack had got the slug out and it was healing well. He helped Jed to his feet.

'You need a stiff drink,' he said. 'We

both do. How about you, Hetty? Coming along?'

When they were seated in the Belle Fourche saloon Lawson looked at the silent, disconsolate widower.

'You know I feel somehow to blame for this. I shoulda checked out this joint when we first reached town to make sure there were no badhats around. Only I went to buy myself a carbine. And, I was kinda peckish, I must admit. Then, if I hadn't started firing . . . Hell I shoulda yelled at you both to hit the deck, but in the heat of the moment I forgot.'

'Don't blame yourself, Mr Lawson. No guilt attaches to you.'

'Call me, Bill. So, what you gonna do now, Jed?'

'I told you. I'm going to inform Cassie's family of the awful facts. Then I'm going after her killers.'

'You! You're crazy. You're just a city boy. These men are hardened outlaws. They'll eat you for breakfast.'

'I don't care. I know how to ride. I've

done a bit of hunting, bear and varmints in the woods round my home. I know how to shoot. I'm gonna get me a gun and go after them.' He gulped the whiskey back. 'The sooner I start the better, while the trail's warm.'

Lawson glanced at Hetty, lit a cheroot, and studied its burning tip for a while. 'Look, I'll level with you, Jed. I'm a Remington agency man. I've been on the trail of these boys a long time. I could lead you to their hideout, but getting in there's a different matter. Nobody gets through the Hole-in-the-Wall without their say-so. It's guarded day and night.'

'A Remington man.' Jed turned his blue, boyish eyes on him. 'I thought you were well-armed.'

Bill Lawson grinned and produced his T-shaped Krug automatic from beneath his coat. 'You can forget your old Colt Frontier. This is superior in every way. It cliploads through the grip. Much faster than reloading every slug into the cylinder. See?' He ejected a clip and showed him the long, round-nosed full metal jacket bullets. 'It uses the new European smokeless powder. Gives deep penetration. Light-weight. Easy to carry. State of the art.'

The young man's slim, pale face registered a bitter awe as he examined the proffered weapon. 'Where can I get one of these? Guns! I'll meet them on their own terms. I'll fight fire with fire.'

'You can't. There's a waiting list. They have to be specially ordered. Look, if you're so hell-fire keen to get yourself killed, maybe we should go into this together? As I say, I've been watching out for this gang a long while. I've been posing as a butcher in Rapid City under the alias Bill Laverty. One of these boys, the Winnemucca Kid, robbed the bank there and I went after him. I was hoping to persuade him to get me into the Hole-in-the-Wall, but he was too suspicious. I admit it, I've made a damn balls-up of my mission. I feel badly about it. Your wife was a sweet gal, Mr Long.'

'Yes.' Tears glimmered in Jed's eyes again as he struggled to control himself. 'But, like you say, she's gone. Maybe she wouldn't want me to do this. But I'm determined. So, how do you propose we get into the Hole-in-the-Wall, Mr Lawson?'

'You'd better get used to calling me Laverty. And you'll need a new name. How about Jed Stone? That's easy enough to remember. My idea is we make it look like we're outlaws. The boss of the JC ranch is ready to help. He's had enough of these no-goods on his borders. Maybe we could pretend to help ourselves to some of his cattle, and make a beeline for the Hole with the JC boys hot on our heels?'

'Sounds good. When do we start?'

'The doc says I can take this sling off tomorrow. That soon enough? Come on.' He tossed back his drink, and then reached for the powerful .45 – 70 Springfield carbine. 'It's no use looking at the world through the bottom of a bottle. We're gonna need clear heads.

Let's go buy you some guns.'

'Eugh!' Hetty gave a shiver of distaste. 'Guns! You sure you want to do this, Mr Long? You're in a very emotional state. I don't think you should let Mr Lawson here talk you into doing something you're not ready for.'

'He's not talking me into it, Miss Pace. This is something I gotta do.'

'Guns are still the only way of getting justice done in this old frontier world,' Lawson said. 'Can you suggest any other way, Hetty?'

She shrugged, helplessly. 'I suppose not. I just don't want to see you — him — get killed. To get in with this gang sounds like long odds.' There was deep sympathy in her metal-grey eyes, with their darkly pronounced aureoles about the irises, as she studied the younger man. She reached out and touched his hand. 'I guess all I can say is, take care.'

'Yes, I'm sorry Miss Pace — '

'Hetty.'

'I guess I got to cancel your

appearance at Deadwood. Number forty-four saloon will stay closed. But, who knows, maybe I'll invite you back for a big reunion concert one day.'

'Yeah, we're sorry to miss your show, Het. You putting one on here tonight?' Lawson asked.

'Yes, excerpts from Gilbert and Sullivan. What they called their Sunday pops. I must go and rehearse in the concert hall.' She stood and offered her hand. 'I'm glad my job is to entertain and make people smile. I wouldn't like yours.'

Lawson watched her go. 'Quite a gal.'

'Yes, she is,' Jed murmured. 'She's got a lot of spirit to be out in this wild country on her own.'

In the town gun shop Lawson — or Laverty — examined the stock of revolvers, spinning the cylinders, listening to their click as he held them to his ear, peering along the sights, weighing them for balance in his palm, putting each aside with a down-turned, quizzical grimace. 'Most of these have got a trigger pull as creaky as my aunty's old front gate.'

'If you're looking for something special, sir,' the gunshop owner suggested, taking a short-barrelled, nickel-plated revolver from his glass display cabinet, 'how about this? The Smith and Wesson new model .32. It has a rebounding hammer. It acts as a safety device to prevent the hammer coming into contact with the cartridge at any time except at the instant of intentional discharge.'

'Yeah?' Bill's rugged features lit up. 'There's plenty of cowboys have shot 'emselves in their own foot from a jolt to their gun.' He handed it to Jed. 'How's it feel? Not too heavy, but it's good enough to stop a man. The ideal beginner's handgun.'

'It feels good.' Jed thumbed the hammer, his face deadly serious as he aimed at the wall. 'Yes.'

'Give it a try out back.' Bill filled the cylinder with slugs from a box and followed the owner out to his practice arcade. 'See that centre dummy? Aim for the belt buckle. There ain't much kick to these, but it should jerk you higher. Take your time, aim, fire, aim, fire . . . aim, fire.'

The shots cracked out as Jed extended his right arm from the hip. To him the straw-stuffed dummy was the man who murdered his wife. He let out his breath through gritted teeth when the cylinder was empty. 'There!'

'You certainly put paid to that *hombre*. A cluster of six around the heart. You've got a good eye.'

'From the hip, too.' The gunshop owner sounded impressed. 'It's made for the gentleman. He can't do better. A snip at fifty dollars.'

'We'll give you forty. He'll be needing a rifle, too. I like the look of that Mauser,' Bill said, as they returned to the shop. He took it from the rack, hugged it to his good shoulder, squinted along the sights. 'Too light-weight for me, but a fine weapon. Bolt action. Try it, Mr Stone.'

The young widower smiled for the first time that day. 'Thank you, Mr Laverty.' He drew the well-oiled bolt as the shop owner praised the weapon's merits, the new-fangled 'scope, the stock of European walnut, chequered in the old cut style.

'For the uninitiated,' Bill explained, 'European walnut is far superior to American, being harder, denser and much more handsome.'

'Oddly enough, it was made on licence in Sweden,' the gunsmith said. 'I'd like to meet the Swede who wound up the guard screws on this rifle. I had to use a wrench on the screwdriver to remove them and dismount the stock.'

'Yeah? It's a nice solid piece. OK, we'll take it. A hundred dollars cash, OK? And two cartons of ammunition. And that tooled leather gunbelt. Right. We'll try it out down by the river. You sure you can afford this, Jed?'

'Yes. What else should I do with my cash? I'm on my own now.'

Bill Lawson glanced at him, uneasily.

He had taken his wife's death hard. Was he up to the strain of this mission? Long was a virgin in comparison to the hard men they would meet. But perhaps the blow of Cassie's death had forged and strengthened his resolve. Jed had a cold determination about him. He wanted to see justice done. And he also thirsted for revenge.

'If I swear you in as my deputy,' Bill told him, as they left the gunshop with their purchases, 'you will have licence to kill. But remember, boy, you take orders from me, and you only use that power in the most dire necessity. It's obvious we can't take on the whole gang. But if we can allay their suspicions, worm our way in among them, my plan is to arrest them one or two at a time. Ideally, I want to take them out alive to face trial.'

'That sounds fair enough to me.'

Bill shrugged and grinned, as he tipped his derby over his brow and scratched the back of his head, gently touching the lump still there from

Della's carbine-butt blow. 'Of course, that ain't allus possible. These men are fast and deadly and go for their guns at the slightest provocation.'

'I'll be ready either way.'

'Right. Now I think you oughta get yourself rigged out in some Western clothes. And we'll buy ourselves a couple of half-decent horses and some supplies, and we're ready to go. I'll telegraph the JC Ranch that we're on our way.'

The two men set off on horseback on the trail to Deadwood City and when they reached that cluster of ramshackle, pitch-roofed huts built both sides of the gulch among the pines another funeral service was in progress, that of Sheriff John Wyler.

'You can see we're not dealing with choirboys. Hogan's a man who boasts that no jail can hold him and so far it's proved true.'

★ ★ ★

'So, this is it?' Jed Long said, as he pulled his mustang to a halt in front of number forty-four Deadwood Gulch. A long, timber building had its front doors nailed and barred closed. Above them scrawled on a board in crimson paint was the legend, HANNAH'S DANCE HALL.

'Liquor and prairie nymphs freely available — at a price,' Bill Lawson laughed.

Jed looked around at the hills pitted with discarded mines and stumps of felled pines. 'This is what we came all this way for? This was our dream? This is what Cassie died for?'

'Yeah, it don't look much, does it? Come on, boy. Let's head on.'

8

The outlaws had put about sixty miles between themselves and Deadwood, weaving their way through the Black Hills, and in a roseate dawn mist had reached a natural pool into which a stream of waterfall plunged, as, in these early days of summer, the snow melted on the peaks.

'We oughta hide up here a bit,' the Kid said, as he stepped from his pinto and let it drink and graze.

He looked around him at the dark, silent hills which always imbued him with a strange sense of calm and peace. He gave a shake of his long hair as he took off his hat and touched his amulet. 'You see why the Sioux call this Paha Sapa?'

'What's that?' Della murmured.

'The Sacred Land.'

Even though they too had Indian

blood the Hogans seemed unawed by the scenic beauty. 'Why hang around?' Dan asked.

'Joe's about all in. We gotta get that slug outa him. An' the hosses could do with a rest.'

The Texican had, in fact, been hanging around his bronc's neck, groaning at every jolt to his injured leg. When they stopped by the pool he crawled towards it to drink.

'Too bad.' Donny pulled his revolver and aimed it at the back of Pizanthia's head. 'If he cain't ride he ain't holding me back. Hey, Dan, maybe I should put him outa his pain?'

Pizanthia looked up, fear filling his dark eyes. 'No, don't do this, boys.'

'That's enough.' The Kid's Hopkins had appeared in his hand and he was covering the Hogans. 'If you wanna go, you go. We'll stay with Joe. How about you, Della?'

'I'm with you.'

'Aw, let me breeze him,' Donny said, thumbing his hammer.

'Why's your brother so damn hard? Joe's one of us.'

Dan Hogan gave a roar of laughter. 'We was brought up in Missouri, that's why.'

'That explains it?'

'Sure, that explains it. We had a hard life. Our Mammy and Daddy, they was both kilt. It was me brought Donny up. He's more of a son to me. Thass why we take care of *ourselves*.'

'If you think we're gonna wait for the posse to catch up you got to think again,' Donny snarled. 'Come on, Dan.'

'You three are too damn soft-hearted to be outlaws. That ain't the way you stay alive.' Dan Hogan turned his horse, spurring it away, shouting back. 'See you back at the Hole, if the posse don't git ya.'

'Scumbags,' the Kid muttered, as he studied the hole in Pizanthia's thigh. 'You're lucky, Joe. I don't think it's hit the bone.'

He deftly lit a small fire, boiled up water, washed his scalping knife, shoving a gag into the Texican's mouth so he wouldn't bite off his tongue. 'Hold him down, Della. That's right. Sit on his damn face.' The Kid slid the razor-sharp, horn-handled knife in. Joe's screams of pain were muffled by Della as he gouged deeper. 'Got it,' he hissed, as he dug the lead bullet out. 'Come on,' he slapped Joe's face to bring him round. 'I'm gonna haul you into the pool. You lie there as long as you can. Let the water sluice through the wound. Thass the way the Sioux do it.'

Della hammered coffee beans on a rock, boiled up their tin pot, passed a steaming mug of the black liquid to the Kid. They watched the Tex-Mex lying in the pool, his blood curdling away. 'Underneath you ain't a bad guy, are you, Kid? You're one of the good guys. We didn't ought to be with these men. Why don't we go off on our own?' Della said.

'Heck!' The Kid made a grimace. 'A guy can't leave his pals. Joe'll be OK if the gangrene don't set in. My guess is the posse'll figure we've made a bee-line for the plains. They won't be expecting us to hang about. At least, let's hope so. So relax, Della.'

They baked a flapjack in the ashes of the fire for breakfast and extinguished the smoke as the sun rose high. The Kid made a rod from a bough and a hook from one of Della's hairpins and stood thigh-deep out in the pool fishing for trout. Soon he had a dozen of the rainbow-hued fish cooling for their supper in a rock pool. Their horses grazed on lush grass, and, as it grew hotter, they lazed and splashed about like kids.

'Let's go explorin'.' Della tipped him a saucy wink. So they left Joe lying with his leg in the water.

'Any trouble,' the Kid called. 'Give a holler.'

They followed the stream, climbing through massive mossy rocks and ferns, until they reached the base of the waterfall where it pounded into another pool in a haze of spray.

'It's bakehouse hot here,' Della cried, unbuttoning her blouse and stepping out of her skirt. 'I'm gonna skinny dip.'

He watched her pale, lissom figure as she balanced naked on a rock and jumped into the pool, and swam, sinuous and shiny as a fish, grinning up at him.

'Come on in,' she called.

The Winnemucca Kid glanced about him. It was risky. Any moment one of those vigilante men might turn up. Or even a grizzly. He didn't like being too long apart from his guns. Then he said, 'Hail, why not?' He pulled off his boots, un-notched his gunbelt, dropped his pants, and dived in to join her.

They swam around, hooting and hollering, splashing and snorting in the crystal cold water, bobbing in each other's arms. Della's legs wound around his hips. They kissed, their tongues meeting hungrily, their eyes sparkling with merriment into each other's. Without a word they clambered out on to a flat rock and slid into each other . . .

When they were done they lay on the rock to dry off in the sun. Della snuggled her head into the Kid's shoulder, her fingers caressing his bronzed, muscular chest.

'You know,' she whispered, 'sometimes I think you really do like me. Otherwise, how could a gal be so happy?'

'Quiet,' he snapped, jerking up to support himself on his shoulders, sensing intruders, looking around up at the rocks and the woods. 'Get your clothes.' He reached out stealthily for his carbine. 'I heard something.'

Up in the woods above them Jed Long slid down the slope to join Bill Lawson who was peering over a rock, sighting along his Springfield. Jed looked down the steep cliff and saw a bronzed young black-haired man and a girl lying on a rock, naked as nature intended.

'It's the Kid,' Bill whispered. 'Caught

him with his pants down.'

'Are you going to take him?' Jed was drawing the bolt of his Mauser. 'What about the girl?'

Lawson was taking the first pressure on his trigger, his face intent beneath his derby. 'I could kill him now,' he hissed. 'But, I dunno. Maybe it's best to play 'em along.'

Down below the Kid suddenly rolled for cover behind a rock, lowering himself into the water, levering a bullet into the breech, peering up into the trees of the cliffside.

'Get your head down, gal. There's someone or something up there.'

A rock was hurled down, splashing into the water beside him, and he heard a deep chuckling laugh. 'Look at them two. Who they think they are, Adam and Eve?'

Della slid back into the water beside him, her eyes anxious. 'Who is it?'

'I dunno. But whoever it is they got us pinned down.' He studied a movement in the leaves and squinted along the carbine sights. 'If you want to parley,' he shouted, 'show yourself.'

'It's you who's showing yourself.' Another husky cackle of laughter. 'You better get outa there, Kid, or you'll catch your death of cold.' And a voice began singing, 'Bury me not on the lone prairie . . . where the wild coyotes will howl over me . . . remember me, Kid?'

'The bastard,' the Kid muttered. 'Who is he?'

'It's the damn butcher,' Della said, as she saw a derby hat waved on a rifle barrel from up behind a rock.

'What's he want?'

'Hey, we were gonna be partners, remember?' Lawson roared. 'Throw your carbine out and I'll put mine aside. I coulda killed ya ten minutes ago when you were hard at it. But I enjoyed the show. We're on the lam, like you.'

'We? Who's with him?' The Kid looked at Della who was shivering, her face turning blue. 'Ah, well, it's too damn chilly to stay in here.' He tossed the carbine out on to the rock. 'I guess we gotta take a chance on 'em.'

'There's n-not much else we can do,' Della stammered, as she scrambled out of the water, hugging herself, reaching for her clothes. 'Come on down,' she yelled. 'The more the merrier.'

The 'butcher' slithered down the slope to join them, followed by a slim young fellow, dark-haired, dressed in black shirt and pants, with fringed chaps, tooled leather boots, and spurs. He had a Mauser in his hand, and a .32 revolver in an ammunition-laden gun-belt around his waist.

'Whadda ya want?' The Kid was standing erect, unashamed of his nakedness, only the wooden amulet hanging from his neck. 'Who's he?'

'Waal, whadda ya know? We meet again. This is my new sidekick, Jed Stone. You been stirring up them vigilantes and they're after us now.'

'What for?'

'We stopped the Miles City stage and relieved the passengers of their cash.

One of 'em was the manager of the Belle Fourche bank. And all the time you boys was tryin' to rob his bank. See, I got his gold watch here as a souvenir, for twenty-five years' faithful service.'

Bill Lawson had, in fact, persuaded the bank manager to lend him the watch when he returned to Belle Fourche, explaining his intentions to join the robbers. It would make a convincing cover story. He swung the watch by its chain.

Della caught it and read the engraving on the cover of the case. 'Presented by the Belle Fourche Bank in grateful recognition of loyal service to . . . '

'Yeah?' the Kid said. 'So, whadda ya want?'

'Aw, I thought we'd just ride along together for a bit. Four guns is better than two. You can keep that bay you stole off me.'

'Please yourself,' the Kid said, going to pull on his pants. He stared at Jed Stone, meeting his frank blue eyes, frowning, with a puzzled look. 'Ain't I met you some place?'

'No, I don't believe you have,' Jed replied.

'We got trout for supper.' Della was jerking up her pantalettes over her damp buttocks, her naked breasts bobbing. 'There's plenty to spare for you boys.'

The Kid took another look at Stone, shrugged, buttoned his shirt, loosely knotted his bandanna, picked up his carbine, rammed on his big, bullet-holed hat and led the way to their camp. 'This is Greaser Joe. You better bring your hosses down.'

Bill Lawson winked at Jed as they turned to climb back up the cliff. 'I think they've fallen for it,' he muttered. 'But I ain't so sure the Hogans will be so easily fooled.'

The moon rose from behind the pine-swathed peaks as they lazed around the campfire after devouring the fish supper. Bill Laverty produced a mouth organ from his vest pocket and began to pump out a medley of popular refrains as the others sang along.

'Well, you're certainly better company than them other two,' Della cried. 'He might be a pal of yourn, Kid, but Dan Hogan makes my flesh creep. And the same goes for Donny.'

'Where are they?' Laverty asked.

'Gone on ahead. They were ready to put a bullet in poor ol' Joe.'

'They two bad boys, but that the way it is.' The Latino flashed his gold teeth. He seemed to be in better shape, but weak from loss of blood. 'I will be OK to ride *mañana*.'

'Goodnight, boys,' Della said, rolling up in her blanket. 'I'm plumb wore out.'

'Must be all that swimmin' you were doing,' Laverty laughed.

'You boys can get some shut-eye,' the Kid said, picking up his carbine. 'I'll take first watch.' He stalked away up the mountainside. And the others settled down into their own bedrolls, smoking and talking before they nodded off.

When he slipped back into the circle at about one in the morning Joe was still awake. The Kid poured him a coffee from the pot simmering on the fire.

'What you think of these two?' he asked.

'Sleeping like babes. You could slit their throats now.'

'Yep I guess. But they seem all right.' The Kid kicked at Laverty's rump, and, as he jumped awake, drawled, 'Your turn, old man.'

Bill yawned, drank coffee, picked up his rifle and climbed up into the rocks. The Texican nodded at Della, who was sleeping, a blissful look on her young, hard face in the flickering firelight.

'You know, Kid, she's a nice gal in spite of her profession. She ain't like them other crazy bitches. Della's got a lot of good things going in her head. She's real fond of you. You know, you oughta be nicer to her. She might not be faithful to you in her body, but in her mind I'm sure she is. A man's lucky if he finds a girl like that.'

'A chippy with a heart of gold, eh?' the Kid drawled in a mocking voice, staring at the sleeping girl. 'Della's OK, but I ain't figurin' on gittin' hitched. I told her so. If you want her, Joe, you have her.'

'It ain't right to treat her like that, Kid.'

'So?' He stuck his knife into the ground beside him, and wriggled into his tarpaulin-covered soogan. He stared awhile at the other man, Jed Stone, his handsome features cleanly chiselled, his long lashes over eyes closed in sleep. 'Who's he? That's what puzzles me. Where've I seen him afore?'

'Probably some saloon. Young fellas like him drift in and out.'

'Nope. He ain't from these parts.

Must be someplace else. I tell you what, he's a greenhorn. He ain't used to this kinda life.' He shrugged and settled down, and muttered, 'We gonna have to keep an eye on these two.'

9

The prairie grass, spangled with flowers, was up to their horses' bellies as the five 'outlaws' rode on across the wide Powder River country of Wyoming beneath a sky piled high with cumulus clouds. When they reached the wire of the JC spread the Kid jumped down and attacked it with his cutters. They rode on across the immense range and soon spotted a herd of white-faced Herefords contentedly grazing.

'Hey, what's the hurry to get to the Hole?' Bill Lawson grinned. 'Why not help ourselves to a few of these beauts? I got me a running iron in my saddlebag. JC can soon be doctored to JO. We can say it's a new brand from up Montana way. We can drift 'em down to Rawlings and raise ourselves some pocket money.'

The Winnemucca Kid's blue eyes

studied him, thoughtfully. 'Waal, we ain't been doing so good at bank robbin'. Why not? Let's make a fire, rope a few, and start branding.'

Bill scratched at his rocky chin and adjusted his derby. 'Maybe I should take a ride up towards the ranch-house to make sure the coast's clear. Nobody knows me round here, so if I bump into any of the JC boys I'll just spin 'em a yarn.'

Again, the Kid studied him, but nodded assent. 'Right we'll start rounding up some stock.'

It was, in fact, only about six miles to the JC ranch-house, and Lawson made a beeline across the plain to it. When he met a bunch of cowboys he showed them his badge, and they escorted him in to meet the boss, Bud Freeman.

'We don't want any more funerals so my idea is you all come chasing after me hell-for-leather, your shooting irons blazing, but make sure you don't git too close. We'll set off up into the Big Horns and you can follow. Make it look good but don't take any risks. Those bastards up there are crack shots.'

'Once you're in there,' Freeman asked, 'what you gonna do?'

'We'll play it by ear. Look, I've had a couple of Wanted posters printed about me. Wanted for murder, rape, arson, kidnapping and robbery up in Montana. Quite a badman, eh? That should impress 'em. Once I've got their trust I'll try to get word out about what they're up to.'

'The sooner those rats are smoked outa there the better it will be,' Freeman said. 'They're too near my property.'

The Kid was in the act of burning in a new brand as Della and Jed Long held the heifer down when he heard the sound of gunfire and jumped to his feet. A cloud of dust was being kicked up by about thirty horses' hooves, and he saw the flash of gunfire as they came thundering towards him across the plain. Well out in front was the stocky Remington man, hanging on one-handed to his bronc, slapping his horse with his derby as he rode.

'Aw, shee-it. Let's git outa here. You OK, Joe? *Vamos*, pronto.'

He helped the Texican on to his horse and leaped into the saddle of his pinto, heading for the gap in the wire, and circling back up towards the hills. It was a hard and fast race across the plain, turning in the saddle to fire revolvers at their pursuers, as Bill caught up with them. Their broncs couldn't keep up that pace when they started the steep ascent towards the Hole and they were forced to slow to a jog trot, but spurring and whipping their mounts leaping on up through the rocks.

'They're still following,' Jed said, looking back, but noticing that the ranchmen, too, were finding the ascent a struggle.

It so happened that Ned Hagen, sheriff of Rapid City, with a small posse, had decided to scout the vicinity around the Hole-in-the-Wall and fell in with the JC boys, joining in the chase.

Bud Freeman warned him of the plan, and told him to curb his natural enthusiasm to capture the Kid, not take any chances.

'That sounds like a durn crazy idea to me,' Hagen drawled. 'We oughta try and catch up with this bunch while we got the chance.' And he spurred his mustang on up the slope as the great rocky battlements of the Hole-in-the-Wall hide-out towered over them.

The Hole-in-the-Wall was the entrance to a natural fortress rimmed by steep rugged buttes and bluffs and a thousand-feet high red rock wall to the north side. There were caverns for hiding, passages for escape, and the main entry pass through which no intruder could make his way without riding under the guns of the outlaw sentinels. The narrow gorge, the Hole-in-the-Wall, was the only way in and made the hide-out practically impregnable.

As they climbed their horses up into the Big Horn mountains the land became ever more bleak, the wind whistling across bare craggy slopes, the going ever more hazardous to beast and man.

'Where the hell we going?' Della yelled, pausing to look around. 'It's kinda eerie up here. My pony's about all in, Kid.'

'Leave him. Get on my pinto. We're almost there.' He ducked as a shot whistled past his ear. 'There's some bastard gaining on us.'

'Yeah?' Bill Lawson sounded surprised. 'And he's shooting to kill.'

'What you expect him to do?' the Kid called, as the fugitives scrambled their horses on up to the slit in the wall. Now lead was whining over their heads from the rocks above, aimed at their pursuers. Dan Hogan and the outlaws up in the caves had been alerted by the sound of gunshots and had taken up positions watching the five fugitives being chased up the valley by the posse and cowhands. Now they had started pouring a withering rifle-fire fusillade at the latter.

'Dan certainly ain't putting out the welcome mat,' the Kid grinned as he reached the shadowy slit in the rock. 'Hay-yup!' He made a kissing sound and urged the bay through, followed by Joe, and Della on his pinto.

Sheriff Hagen was indeed shooting to kill, his carbine at his shoulder as he urged his powerful mount on up. One of his slugs chiselled the wall as Jed and Bill waited their turn to go through.

'Durn fool,' Lawson scowled, looking back. 'What's he playing at?'

Hagen saw the last two disappear into the Hole and charged on up.

'Hold your hoss in, sheriff,' old Hank Thompson, the bank guard, shouted. 'It's suicide to follow 'em through there.'

Hagen wasn't listening. He had chased these outlaws a long way. He had a determined scowl on his tanned face. He urged his horse through the dark entranceway and emerged into sunshine. He looked up the slope to a main cavern overhang where a wall of rocks had been built up as a barrier. Men were crouched behind it, the sun gleaming on their weapons. The run-aways were climbing up to it on foot, leading their horses. He took all this in in the space of a second and didn't like the look of it at all. But he was committed now, and he raised his carbine and aimed at the back of the Winnemucca Kid.

Dan Hogan had his sights lined up on the brightly shining tin star on the sheriff's chest. 'Pow!' A bullet powered out and hit an inch below, spouting a gout of blood and the lawman was catapulted from his saddle.

'Thar's one for the pot,' he yelled.

Hank, too, abandoned caution, charging through the dark slit with the wild instincts of an old frontiersman. Donny Hogan's carbine slug slammed between his bronc's eyes and he crumpled instantly dead. Hank rolled clear and crawled for the cover of a rock. He kept his head down as bullets chiselled about him. 'Hot damn,' he growled, as he looked across at the sheriff's lifeless body. 'I warned him. How'm I gonna git outa here? These boys don't play for peanuts.'

Hank climbed arthritically to his feet as the fugitives scrambled into the cave and he saw the sheriff's startled horse wandering back towards him. He grabbed at the saddle horn and hauled himself aboard, groping for the reins.

Up in the cave Bill Lawson saw Dan Hogan aim his rifle at old Hank's back as he headed down towards the gap in the rocks. He pretended to slip and grabbed at Hogan's shoulder as he fired. The shot went wild and Hank squeezed his mount back through to safety.

'What the hell you doin'?' the 'Gorgon' roared, pushing Bill off.

'Sorry, mister,' Bill grinned. 'These rocks are devilish for high-heeled boots.'

'Kid, where the hell you find this ninny? What you brung him here fer?'

'Aw, Bill's OK. He's got form. You should see that Wanted bill they got out on him. This other one, too. They both on the run. We were gonna steal some JC stock but they got on our tails. Seems like a rustler cain't make a dishonest living no more.'

While the rest of the outlaws kept up a hail of fire on the posse, who had taken cover in the rocks beyond the gap, Hogan peered wild-eyed at the poster and the likeness of 'Laverty', and growled, 'You ain't been wastin' your time up in Montana by the looks of this. Welcome to the Hole, pal. We can do with a couple more guns. We've had some losses of late.'

Bill had had a bill printed for Jed, too, who took the crumpled article from his shirt pocket and presented his credentials. 'I killed a man in Sioux City over some gal — he kinda caught me in bed with her — and I've been on the run since. Holding up stagecoaches is my speciality, as you see.'

'Aw, that's outa date. Small-time

stuff. Robbing trains is where the money's at these days. That's what we're getting into. If you can shoot you're welcome along, son.'

The sulphurous fumes of gunsmoke filled the cave as Hogan's men kept on firing. He glanced down at the pursuers who had retreated down the slope.

'Hold your fire, men. You're wasting ammo. Them assholes ain't got a hope in hell of gettin' up here. Yee-haugh! I killed myself another sheriff. I gotta celebrate. Where's that jug?'

The Hogan brothers had run into a bull-whacker and his team, soon as steam took over to become a thing of the past. He was making his way up the old Bozeman Trail with a wagon-load of whiskey from Laramie. The trail wound up past the burned timber posts of what once had been Fort Reno, across Powder River and Crazy Woman Creek and the sites of the Fetterman and Wagon Box fights, and other bloody battlefields like the Little Big Horn massacre, on for hundreds of miles to

Virginia City, Montana. They had relieved him of a couple of barrels and tied them to their broncs. 'What am I gonna tell my boss?' the whacker wailed.

'Tell him they fell off the back of the wagon,' Hogan had laughed, creasing his hair with a pistol shot.

He poured the newcomers stiff shots, although Jed Long, who didn't much like to drink, nearly choked on the fiery stuff, and discreetly drained his tin mug into the dust.

'Say, you ain't no hard man.' A man called Harry Holm's mad, staring eyes were fixed on Lawson. 'I seen you in Rapid City. You're nuthin' but a durn butcher. What's your game, Mr Lavatory?'

'Laverty,' Bill corrected. 'I was released from Laramie prison on parole on condition I behaved myself. Sure, I tried butchering for six months but it didn't pay enough. So, here I am.'

'It so happens I just bust outa Laramie prison. How come I never saw you in there?'

'When did they throw you in?'

'Last November.' The shaven-headed New Yorker, Holm, had earned the soubriquet Mad Dog Harry with a string of killings, and scowled suspiciously.

'That explains it, pal. I was released in September.'

'So, how come they didn't hang you with all this — rape, arson, murder? Tell me that, Mr Shithole.'

'Because that was up in Montana, dimbrain. I got tried here in Wyoming for a spot of rustling. I was trying to go straight, but I needed some beef for my shop. I guess that's why the governor was lenient. He's a bit weak in the head.'

'Yeah? Well, I heard he's a red hot law and order man. And them guards in Laramie never showed me any leniency. All I got was a clubbing with their billy sticks. I tell you, Hogan, I don't like the sound of this monkey. Something stinks.'

'Hell, they showed us their references, ain't they?' Like most criminals, Hogan was mightily impressed by a man's 'form', and, to tell the truth, he was already too whiskeyed-up to care. 'We can give 'em a trial, cain't we? Who's running things here?'

'I tell you what, Mad Dog,' Donny put in. 'If these two ain't right they'll live to regret it. I'll be watchin' 'em like a hawk. One step outa line and' — he drew his thumb across his throat — 'Yeuk!'

'Yeah, Donny's got strong feelings about spies and informers. Shooting's too good for 'em,' Hogan laughed. 'He likes to break their fingers one by one.'

'They're pulling out,' an old soldier, Pegleg Peebles, still wearing a faded forage cap, yelled. 'The chickens have had enough. They're turning tail.'

The bandits whooped and sent a volley of lead whistling and careering down the rocky canyon as the cowboys and possemen climbed on their horses and headed away. Mad Dog bounded down to strip the dead sheriff of his guns, boots and cash, leaving his body half-naked for the buzzards and eagles to feed on. And, as night fell, they set to demolishing the barrels of whiskey.

Soon Della was being pestered by their amatory advances as they danced and staggered around the flames. Jed Long looked on uneasily as they grappled with the girl, several times dragging her off into the shadows of side-caves. Wasn't the Winnemucca Kid supposed to be her beau? Why didn't he stop them? But he was busy dealing a greasy pack of cards to the stumpy man with the gargantuan head, Dan Hogan. Huge, grotesque shadows were slopped by the flames against the cave walls. It seemed to him like a scene from Dante's *Inferno*, like a horde of lusty, whiskey-crazed devils wassailing. How would they ever be able to arrest any of these homicidal maniacs, let alone get out of there with their own lives intact?

Suddenly there was a piercing scream from the end of the cave. Della was fighting off Harry Holm, who was trying to drag her towards a cave.

'Keep your hands off me,' she shrieked. 'I'm not having *you* touch me.' She reached out for a discarded bottle and smashed it over his head. Holm stood there dazed for seconds, brushing glass from his stubbled skull. Della was holding the jagged bottle-neck, threatening him.

'You would, would you, you bitch,' he yelled, and twisted the weapon from her hand. He slashed it at her face. If she hadn't jerked her head back her nose would have been severed. As it was, his reverse slash spurted blood from across her top lip. He had her by the hair and was aiming at her jugular, hand-raised, when a shot cracked out, a bullet slicing his hand.

'Aagh!' Holm cursed as he dropped the bottle stump, and turned sucking at his knuckles. 'You — '

'Yeah, me.' The Kid was standing with his smoking Allen and Hopkins pointed at him. 'Leave the girl alone.

She don't want you. Nobody wants you. You're just city trash.' He spun the revolver on his finger, slipped it back into his holster, splayed his fingers over the butt. 'Come on, Holm, try me.'

Holm's bloody paw started towards the Colt stuck in his belt. 'How can I?' he whined. 'Look what you done to my hand.'

'Consider yourself lucky.'

Holm pointed a finger of his good hand. 'Watch it, boy. I'm gonna settle with you soon, I swear. And her, too.'

The Kid shrugged and returned to the game, as Della came to sit beside him, staring at the blood on her hand pouring from her cut lip. 'He's crazy,' she whispered. 'He was going to kill me. I could see it in his eyes.'

'Aw, why you allus causin' trouble?' The Kid flashed a smile at her. 'Here, wash some whiskey over your lip.'

'You better watch out for Holm,' Joe Pizanthia said. 'He's a back-shooter. He don't play by the rules. And you, too, Della.'

'Yeah, you shoulda finished him, Kid,' Hogan growled. 'You're too damn soft.'

'Yeah, if you don't git him, he'll git you,' Donny agreed. 'That guy's a real snake in the grass.'

10

'Welcome to Laramie, gentlemen. I'm glad you all responded to my invitation. I believe we've got to make a joint effort to clean up Wyoming, and your territories, too, in time for the new century. The day of these badmen terrorizing our communities is over. I have made a pledge to my voters that by the start of the year 1900 they will be able to ride free of the fear of molestation.'

The Governor of Wyoming was addressing a meeting in his office of the governors of Utah, Idaho, South Dakota, and their sidekicks, law enforcement officers, and representatives of the Adams Express Company, the American Bankers' Association, and the Union Pacific Railroad.

'Sure, Governor, there's no need to give us your election speech. We're all aware of the facts,' a man called Jack McIntosh butted in. He was the founder of the Remington Detective Agency, set up in Denver, Colorado, in opposition to the more famous Pinkerton one. 'The trouble is these bad boys operate in the Three Corners. They know this wild country like the back of their hands and they can skip away across your borders after they hit. My idea is that it is time you all acted in unison by agreeing to an interstate operation. That's why we've asked you gents from the banks and railroads to give us your support.'

The Wyoming governor banged his fist on his desk and ranted on, 'I intend to bring law and order to the West. For too long these outlaws have had it their own way. For twenty years they've been riding roughshod over us and given our four territories a reputation for lawlessness second to none. I intend to see every lawbreaker shot or hanged or sent down for life.'

'Well, we've busted the big boys.' McIntosh had a sharp, intelligent face and sported a white mane of hair and a bushy walrus moustache. 'Thangs got too hot for them. They showed us a clean pair of heels. Rumour is they're down in Texas, or even planning to start afresh in Argentina. But they left a nucleus of hangers-on who have been giving us problems. They're still holed up in the Hole-in-the-Wall. It's all but impossible to flush the rats outa there. Posses have tried and failed. What I plan to do is infiltrate them, get information of when and where they plan to strike and hit them hard when they do.'

'We've heard all this before,' a little bald-headed accountant from the Bankers' Association put in. 'Have you any idea how many hundreds of thousands of dollars have been stolen from banks and railroad strongboxes in the past ten years?' He looked at his papers and began to detail various raids.

'That's why we've called this meeting,' McIntosh said angrily. 'We want you all to put in hard cash to support the setting up of a super-posse, hand-picked men, top-shootists, who know the terrain, to be installed in a special train here in Wyoming, with fast horses ready to be loaded into the boxcar, so they can steam at top speed immediately to wherever there's trouble. That's the only way we're going to catch these varmints.'

'We're prepared to provide the train and engine, the drivers and accommodation,' a spokesman from the Union Pacific said, 'if you gentlemen will chip in to pay for the expenses of these hired guns. I imagine they don't come cheaply.'

'It's the job of the Adams Express Company to get valuable consignments of cash, gold and silver transported in our armoured cars across the country,' the representative of the company informed the meeting. 'We've taken a hiding at the hands of the outlaws.

We're ready to chip in to whatever it costs.'

When the other three governors and the rest of the men present had noisily indicated their support, the Wyoming governor banged his fist again and said, 'So, that's agreed. We'll get down to hammering out the cost of the operation in due time, but no expense will be spared. Meantime, let's hear from McIntosh just who it is we're after.'

'Right.' The Remington bureau chief took some photographs from his briefcase and tossed them on to the table. 'This here's the leader of the Hole-in-the-Wall gang. Dan Hogan. Yes, ugly-looking animal, isn't he? A natural born killer, if ever there was one. Him and his brother, Donny. No, he's not much better looking, is he? They're ignorant as pig-shit, but they're cunning and ruthless. We believe they've recently been joined by the notorious New York criminal, Harry Holm. He broke out of Fort Laramie prison, killing a guard, and headed for the hills. Mad Dog Holm they call him. They're all cold-blooded psychopaths. We're talking about very dangerous men.

'I got news in on the wire. The Hogan brothers are now wanted for the killing of Sheriff Wyler, of Deadwood, and Sheriff Hagen, of Rapid City. An innocent young bystander, Mrs Cassie Long, was murdered by them, too.'

There was an outcry from those present. The Wyoming governor shouted above them, 'This is too much. This shows we've got to act and hit 'em fast and hard.'

'Who are these others?' the South Dakota governor asked, examining the prison mug-shots.

'The hardcore of the bunch. Those with convictions. Joe Pizanthia, wanted for bank robberies in Texas and New Mexico. Tom O'Leary, Muddy Waters, Deaf Charley Sparrow, Cherokee Williams, they're the ones we know. The rest are just riff-raff.'

'Who's this?'

'Winnemucca Kid, he calls himself. We don't know his real name. Robbed a bank in Rapid City by unorthodox means. A bit of a joker, good-looking half-breed, popular with the ladies. A deadly accurate shot, but not a dyed-in-the-wool killer like the others. At least, not yet. Just a wild young buckaroo.'

'Who's the girl?'

'Della Rose Smith, alias Cleopatra Jenkins. Aged twenty-three, five feet three, buxom build, sallow complexion, prominent teeth. Arrested for passing forged bank notes but released. Several fines for prostitution. Was with the gang on the Belle Fourche raid.'

'So where is this so-called Hole-in-the-Wall gang now, Mr McIntosh? And what are you doing about them?'

'I've had a message from one of my agents, Bill Lawson, that he's infiltrated the gang. He's a good man. But until we get a proper posse set up our hands are tied. These outlaws operate over a vast area in the four territories. They are hard men, used to riding long distances. Searching for them is like looking for a needle in a haystack. And if things get too hot they high-tail it down to Colorado or the Canyon Lands. They generally have fresh horses stashed at strategic points, in deserted canyons, or at small farmsteads of friends.'

'They undoubtedly terrorize the population,' the Wyoming governor said. 'I doubt if they have many real friends. The sooner we get this super-posse set up the better it will be. They won't have any friends then. I believe we should put a price on all of these outlaws' heads, alive or dead. Preferably dead. Hot lead's the only language these rats understand. Is it agreed we furnish our agents with state-of-the-art high-powered weapons, and we give them licence to kill?'

The meeting vociferously agreed, and so the Wyoming governor signalled to his secretary to bring in the refreshments, the whiskey and cigars. 'We're gonna beat these boys,' he said. 'Gentlemen I propose a toast — to the demise of the Hole-in-the-Wall gang.'

11

'Train robbin', that's what we gotta get into,' Dan Hogan said. Over the next few weeks, as Joe Pizanthia rested up his leg, he dispatched Cherokee Williams, Deaf Charley, Peg Leg and the Kid to scout the railroad towns and pass bribes around among engineers, conductors and bank messengers for any information that might be useful. 'Our communal chest is getting low,' he announced, handing out fistfuls of dollars from the tin trunk he kept in his cave. 'We gotta restock soon.'

'There ain't a great deal to do,' Jed muttered to Bill Lawson. 'This sitting around with time on our hands is getting on my nerves. When are we going to act?'

'Just bide your time, boy. Practise your shooting, do a bit of whittling. There's no way we can take on these three psychopaths and twenty other men. We'll strike, as they say, when the iron's hot.'

Jed had found himself a small cave to lay out his bedroll. He didn't much care for the crude company of the other men, and he preferred to be alone with his thoughts. 'I don't know,' he sighed. 'Why can't we just kill the Hogans and have done with it?'

'Easy, Jed. Don't go getting itchy-fingered. You and me, we'll do this properly and we'll ride outa here when this is done. You gotta stay cool, mix more with the men, see what you can — '

He broke off as Della appeared in the doorway of the cave. 'Hi, gal, how's it goin'?'

'What you two chawin' the cud about?'

'Aw, Jed's a bit bored. He's frettin' for action. I'm just explaining that it's like being in the army being with a mob like this. Long periods of lying low, and then — Pow!'

'Maybe I could cheer you up, honey.' Della parted her prominent teeth and waggled her tongue tip at the young man. 'I'm kinda bored myself now the Kid's gone.' She sat down on the ledge of rock beside him and cosied up, coiling an arm around his neck. 'You wanna have fun with me?'

'No!' There was a sharpness to Long's tone as he shook her off, his pale wolfish face tense. 'No thanks.'

'What's the matter? Why so melancholy? Why don't you ever join in the fun like the other boys?'

'Drop it, Della,' Bill growled. 'Jed lost his sweetheart back in Sioux City. That's why he killed that guy. He ain't got over it yet.'

'Oh, I see. Too bad. But you cain't grieve for ever. An' there's me thinkin' he thinks himself too good for me.'

'*I'*m not averse to a bit of fun, Della,' Lawson said, reaching out and pulling her on to his own knee. 'You know, they tell me there used to be as many as two hundred men holed up in these caves.

There's a good many of 'em reaped their reward at the end of a rope, filled with buckshot, thrown in jail, or chased outa the territory. I hear some of 'em even joined Teddy Roosevelt's Rough Riders to go fight in the war with Spain. Hasn't it occurred to you you've chosen the wrong profession?'

'Aw, I like being an outlaw,' she said.

'Let's take a stroll,' he said, winking at Jed and easing her out of the cave. Della hung on to him, and they went to the cliff edge to look out. It was getting dark, the stars popping on.

'You know,' said Lawson, 'if you turned state's evidence, told all you know, you would probably only go down for six months.'

'Aw, I couldn't turn in my pals.'

'Think about it.'

'You're odd, Bill,' Della murmured, snuggling into him, her fingers stroking his rocky jaw. 'You're strong and tough, but you're gentle, too. You don't really belong with these boys, either. What are you doing here? You're not a cold-hearted killer like . . . like Hogan. He would kill you and me if he heard us talking like this.'

'He is what he is. He's riding for a fall. Me, I'm gonna get myself a bankroll and get out. I've had a few rough breaks. It's time I got myself organized, got myself a little spread someplace. I'd like you along. I'm serious, Della.'

'Yes,' she whispered, kissing him. 'I believe you are. I dunno. I'm really the Kid's gal. I'll have to think about it. Let's go lie down in your cave.'

* * *

They were men used to riding long distances and when they left the Hole-in-the-Wall and the Big Horn mountains of central Wyoming they headed south-west, a hundred miles to the cattle town of Rawlins, another hundred to Muddy Gap, on another hundred until they reached the Union Pacific Railroad going straight as an arrow east to west across the plain, the great trans-continental coming from Chicago, through Cheyenne and weaving its way on across the Rockies to San Francisco. It so happened there was a spiral of smoke on the horizon, and as the locomotive drew nearer there was a clanging of the bell, the gasping thrust of the pistons, the rhythmic clatter of the wheels, and their horses shied away as the coaches of the Pullman sleepers, the baggage cars, thundered by. The engineer sounded his steam whistle, 'Wha-whaaaaaaa!' — and the passengers at the windows peered out at the hard-looking men and a girl, with their remuda of spare mustangs, and probably thought they were just a clutch of wandering cowhands, not a gang of notorious desperadoes.

Jed Long, not the most expert of horsemen, had difficulty hanging on to his terrified bronc. It reared, flailing its hooves, as the locomotive thundered by. But the other city dude, Mad Dog Holm, was faring even worse, hanging around his horse's neck as he was almost thrown. The other outlaws wheeled their broncs with the grace of the true Westerners, holding them steady. They rode like centaurs, deep in the saddle, going with the motion, as if horse and man were one. In fact, they seemed happier in the saddle than on foot. Jed, saddle-sore, his bones aching from the hundreds of miles of riding, scowled as he managed to control his feisty beast.

'Where the hell we going?' he asked.

'Rock Springs,' Hogan shouted. 'We jest follow the railroad west.'

'How we gonna stop one of them thangs?' Donny asked.

'There's ways,' Hogan said, watching the train go. He had brought a dozen of his men with him and left a skeleton guard at the Hole. 'This time we'll use explosives. I told the Kid to buy what we needed. He reckons he knows how to use 'em.'

★　★　★

Much of the trouble in Wyoming had been caused by the powerful Stockgrowers' Association bringing in hired killers to cow sod-busters and small ranchers who were eating away at the edges of their lands. The cattle barons had viciously opposed any attempt at organization or unionization by their cowhands, who were mostly laid off in winter, and calling for a better deal. It had all exploded in the brief but bitter Johnson County War when the rustler, Cattle Kate Watson, had been hanged.

The terrible drought of '83, and the devastating winter of '86 – '87, when blizzards left dead cattle littering the plains had added to the problem. Even big ranchers had faced total wipe-out, and their cowboys found themselves out of work. There was little else to do but turn to rustling cattle and horses, robbing stages and banks. The railroads had brought in fugitive scum from the cities like Harry Holm, and, one way or another, for the past twenty years

Wyoming and its surrounding territories had become a hotbed of crime.

'In some ways you can't blame these guys for going to the bad,' Bill Lawson muttered as he explained the situation to Jed around the campfire one night. 'To tell the truth sometimes I got a sneaking admiration for their freebootin' ways.'

'What about Cassie's wasted young life?' Jed demanded, hotly. 'You admire 'em for that?'

'Aw, no,' Bill sighed. 'Course not. But you don't get it, do you? There's good and there's bad in most of us.'

'As far as I can see, the Hogans and Harry Holm are pure evil,' said Jed. 'The sooner we take 'em out, or see 'em hanged, the better it will be.'

'Don't let your bitterness consume you, boy. It don't do no good.'

*　　*　　*

Rock Springs, away out on the western edge of Wyoming, a fuelling stop on the railroad before it began its big climb over the Rockies, was a collection of tumbledown shanties, its citizens grown used to gangs of ruffians riding in to hurrah the town and paint the saloons red, often with blood. The rule of law was practically non-existent. But the storekeepers stayed to service the free-spending outlaws. They didn't question too closely whether their cash was honestly or nefariously come by.

When Hogan's bunch hit town they saw Peg Leg excitedly waving from the sidewalk. 'Hey, boss, them bribes paid off,' he yelled. 'We got a big one.'

Dan smacked him about the face with his hat. 'Just you wait 'til we git in the saloon and over in the corner outa earshot. There ain' no use tellin' the whole town.'

They called for whiskey and joined the Kid at a corner table. 'OK, give us the griff.'

'It's big. The Flyer, on its way back from 'Frisco. It'll be carrying fifty thousand smackeroos in the armoured-car safe. We'll be rich.'

'Is this right?' Hogan demanded, eyeing the Kid.

'Seems like it,' the Kid drawled. 'He got it from the horse's mouth, the conductor who'll be on board with it.'

'Where did you meet this conductor?'

'In Medicine Bow. His name's Flanagan.' Peg Leg looked pleadingly at Hogan. 'This is the real thing, Dan. We got it all worked out. You know that Sugar Loaf Mountain and what they call Thunder Gorge about ten miles west of here? The train slows to cross the bridge. Thass where we could hit. That's on Thursday.'

'What, tomorrow?'

'No, Thursday.'

'So, today's Wednesday, lunkhead.'

'No, it's Tuesday.'

'I know what day it is.'

'I thought it was Friday,' Donny offered.

'Dang me, I could have sworn it was Sunday,' the Kid put in. 'Church bell was chimin' just now.'

'No, that's for a funeral for that cheatin' buzzard Cherokee had to kill. It's Monday. Anybody knows that.'

'Aw, fer Chrissakes.' Hogan began hammering on the table with rage. 'What day is it?' he screamed at the barkeep.

'Waal.' The 'keep desultorily studied the news-sheet he was reading. 'It says here Wednesday, June the fifth. But that was a week ago. Let's see, it was the church social on Monday. Yes, it must be Wednesday.'

'I'm glad we got that sorted out,' Bill grinned. 'You boys work out your plan. I'm gonna go get me some cigars.'

'I'll come with you,' Della said, catching hold of his arm.

She had fitted herself out in Levi jeans, boots and spurs, a yoked shirt, and a gunbelt with a Colt Peacemaker in the holster. She wore a check lumberjacket to hide her womanly shape, and, with her hair tucked into her Stetson, she looked like any lithe young cowboy.

'Hey, folks'll think I'm one of those,' Bill said, disentangling himself. 'I got my reputation to think of. You can't go pawin' me when you're in that get-up. Stay here. I'll only be a few minutes.'

Hogan watched him saunter from the saloon, pushing through the batwing doors. He sniffed and shook his big hairy head like a dog who's been swimming. He got to his feet. 'I'll be back in a minute. I'm gonna git me some of them ceegars, too.'

The wide main street was practically deserted, for most honest folks gave the troublesome town a wide berth. There were shootings most days among the rowdy bandits who had taken to haunting it, and a hullaballoo most of the nights. Hogan saw Laverty disappear into the billiards hall. But, by the time he had got there there was no sign of him inside. 'Didn't a guy wearing a derby just come in here?' he demanded.

'Yeah, he bought a handful of cigars

and went out back to the privy.'

Hogan went out to the privy and peered inside. It was empty, only flies buzzing about its ripe stench.

He scratched at the back of his shaggy head as he returned to the street. 'That's funny. Where's he gone?'

Suddenly he saw Laverty emerge from the post office at the other side of the street. Hogan hurried across, his little legs working overtime. He caught up with Laverty, grabbed him by the arm, and spun him round.

'What you been doin' in there?'

'In where?' Bill's little grey eyes glimmered as he looked down at him. 'The post office? What's it to do with you?'

'You're in my gang.' Hogan stumped his finger into Laverty's belly. 'What you do is my business. You been sending a telegraph, aincha?'

'No, I ain't. As a matter of fact I been wiring some cash to my wife and kid back East. I send 'em some whenever I can. How else they goin' to eat?'

'You married? I didn't know that.'

'Quit pokin' me, will ya, Dan? Yeah, it was a long time ago.'

'Didn't work out, eh?'

'Naw, I've never had much luck with wimmin.'

'Nor me, neither.'

'That's the way it is. This kinda lifestyle. A woman needs to be loved.' Bill put a finger to his eye as if to stifle a tear. 'It allus cuts me up to think about my li'l daughter gal. She'll be about eleven now. Hardly ever seen her daddy. I wonder if she ever thinks of me?'

'Shucks! I dunno. Don't take it so hard, pal. I know what you mean. Come on, you need a drink.'

When they got back to the saloon and sat sipping tumblers of rum, Hogan patted Bill's shoulder and said, 'You know, I'm gonna give you a thousand dollars to send your family after this heist.'

'Send *who*?' Della asked, her ears pricking up.

'His family. Bill does the decent thing. He looks after 'em. He's solid as a rock.'

'I didn't know he had a family.'

The Kid flashed a smile at Della. 'You don't know everything, gal.'

'OK, let's get back to our plan. You know that trestle bridge over the canyon the railroad crosses on the crest of Sugar Loaf Mountain? We'll hit there. Kid, you got the dynamite?'

'Yeah, sorta.'

'What do you mean, sorta?'

'I couldn't get dynamite. They'd run out. So I've got nitroglycerine. I've got six bottles of it.'

'Six bottles? Nitro? Jeez! Are you crazy? You drop a bottle of that you'll blow us all to smithereens.'

'I ain't gonna drop it,' the Kid smiled, wagging a finger. 'I'm an expert with this. I treat it very carefully.'

'What am I?' Hogan mopped at his brow and gasped out the words. 'Surrounded by idiots? Can't anybody do anything right?'

12

A telegram boy in a pillbox hat and uniform went racing through the cattle town of Cheyenne, Wyoming, on his new bicycle. This velocipede was suddenly all the rage. It was forecast that it would put the horse out of business. It didn't need feeding, didn't die on you, and could go at twenty-five miles an hour down hill, almost equal to a horse at full gallop. Of course, a tarmacadam surface was preferred, it wasn't much fun up hills, and, if you were unfortunate enough to get a puncture in your pneumatic tyre, that was a problem. But for fast deliveries in town it was ideal.

The boy went tearing up to an ornate railway carriage, with its own Puffing Billy engine idling, and a horse wagon on the other end. He hammered on the carriage door.

'Mr McIntosh — telegram!'

The Remington Detective Agency chief, with his hair parted centrewise, and his matching walrus moustache, poked his head out, took the telegram, read through it, then flicked the boy a nickel.

'No reply.'

Inside the carriage there were six men, some seated on the edges of double bunks running both sides of the carriage, others lounging with their boots up. They were neatly dressed, mostly with soft shirt and tie beneath their jackets, cleanshaven, and every one was packing a sidearm, with a high-powered rifle close at hand. Naturally, being Westerners, they had wide-brimmed hats on their heads, which they wore indoors and out.

The white-haired McIntosh studied the cable: FLYER FROM FRISCO TO BE HIT BY HOGAN TOMORROW AT SUGAR LOAF MOUNTAIN STOP — B.L.

'Good news, boys. Hogan's planning to hit The Flyer. I want the hosses loaded and ready to roll an hour before sun-up. Any questions, Joe?'

'We're ready to roll whenever you say so. The boys are ready for some action.'

Joe Dafoe was not so dapper as the others, attired more like a cowhand, lean and wiry in a plain shirt buttoned at the throat, piebald waistcoat, batwing chaps and spurred boots. But he was a famous range detective who had tracked many a criminal down.

'Sounds good,' he said.

'You're to meet The Flyer and pounce on the whole gang. I don't want any mistakes this time. Shoot to kill, take no prisoners.'

'We have your authority for that?' Dafoe drawled. 'What if they offer to surrender?'

'Accept and then shoot them. That's the governor's orders. This is total war.'

'What about the money on their heads?'

'You split it among your boys.'

'What about Lawson?'

'Well, obviously, you don't shoot

him. He'll be wearing his trademark derby. But he'll have to take care of himself.'

'And the girl? Shoot her, too?'

McIntosh shrugged. 'That's the way it goes.'

* * *

'Here's to the success of the Wyoming Train Robbers' Syndicate.' Dan Hogan beamed widely with black tobacco-stained teeth. He spat away the cork of a bottle of rum and drank deep. 'Let's liquor. We got a busy day tomorrow. We gonna be more famous than Jesse James.'

'I can't wait to get rich,' Bill 'Laverty' grinned. 'What's your plan?'

'You'll see.' Dan tapped his gargantuan brow knowingly. 'Me an' the Kid got it all worked out.'

'Holy Lucifer!' The Kid spotted a tall man, dressed more urbanely than most in gambler's outfit, cross-over vest, sporting a gold fob-chain, strolling into the saloon. 'If it ain't Matthew Turner! What you doin' here, Mr Turner?'

'Do I know you? Your face rings a bell.'

'Yeah, you're the travelling preacher. You used to hold services in Winnemucca. I was only a kid. You come to preach in Rock Springs?'

'Don't talk crazy,' Hogan growled. 'Matt's on the payroll. He's one of us. He's on the lam, like us all.'

'I'm still a believer in our polygamous faith, but I'm afraid I'm guilty of dipping my hands into the community chest in more ways than one' — he glanced at Della's swelling bosom beneath her shirt — 'and the elders cast me out. Nice to see you, son. How's your folks?'

'Ain't seen 'em since I was fifteen.'

'You ought to send 'em a postcard sometime.'

'Give him a bottle,' Hogan said. 'Underneath his fancy talk your friend preacher here's sought in Salt Lake City for swindling the Mormons outa thousands of dollars. And, on top of that, he raided a mining camp and killed a man. He's wanted for homicide. There's a price on his head.'

'I'm afraid I panicked. It was regrettable.' Turner bowed and raised Della's fingers to his lips. 'Such beauty among such beasts.'

'Who you calling a beast?' Hogan snarled, taking another glug of the bottle. 'I need this stuff. It's like oxygen to me. How's the saloon going, Matt?'

'It's all but ready. I've used our cash wisely, imported furnishings from Omaha, walnut bar, velvet curtains, poker table, which I'll tend, imported a piano-player and his instrument. All we need now are some gals.'

'Well, you ain't got much of a choice here,' the Kid drawled, glancing at the four assorted prairie nymphs, their painted faces sticky with sweat, who were being waltzed around the bar floor by Hogan's randy men. 'Della's about the best of the bunch, and that ain't sayin' much.'

'Watch your mouth,' the girl said. 'Why do you allus have to be so mean? I might tell you, in your absence Bill's more or less proposed to me.'

'He has?' the Kid smiled. 'What the hell fer?'

'Well, it ain't official yet.' Bill waggled his hand back and forth and changed the subject. 'Where is this new saloon of your's, Matt?'

'Eagle Valley. I've refurbished an abandoned ranch house. It's going to be the ritziest sporting house west of Cheyenne.'

'Eagle Valley?' Joe Pizanthia protested. 'Thass miles from anywhere. Who gonna be your customer?'

'We are, Joe,' Hogan said. 'It's gonna be our secondary hide-out to the Hole. It's right on the Three Corners — Wyoming, Utah, Idaho — we can pop across the line any time. This joint is OK, but it's on the railroad and undefendable. Eagle Valley's the perfectest location. When you gonna open, Matt?'

'Anytime. I've brought the wagon in to collect some booze.'

'Make it tomorrow night. We'll have us a ball.'

* * *

Sugar Loaf mountain reared brilliant white against a clear blue sky. Below it was a deep and wide chasm through which a fast river flowed. Across this a scaffold bridge had been built of hundreds of lodgepole pines to provide a crossing for the railroad. Hogan and his men stood on the western side the next morning watching with interest the Winnemucca Kid swinging like an agile cat from pole to pole beneath the bridge. At certain points he halted to wrap his legs around a pole and carefully string a bottle of nitroglycerine to the underside of the track. He clambered on his way, seemingly unperturbed by the yawning space beneath, a drop of hundreds of feet to the torrent rushing through

160

the rocks below.

'Hi,' he grinned as he reached them and climbed up the bank. 'Got a drop of that for me?'

'Nope.' Hogan swallowed the last drop of Red Eye and tossed the bottle into the chasm. 'You need a steady hand.'

'This is child's play.' Winnemucca went to pick up the three remaining bottles of nitro that he had left in a canvas bag behind a rock. He stumbled as he picked one up.

'Whoops!' He juggled and caught it. 'Nearly blowed us all to Heaven's Gate,' he grinned, as he held the bottle up. 'Who wants to argue with me?'

'For the Lord's sake!' Bill Lawson breathed out deep. 'Just be careful with that stuff.'

The Kid put the bag over his shoulder and swung on to his pinto to ride alongside Jed as they followed the others over the ridge beneath the gleaming white cone of Sugar Loaf mountain.

'You know, you and me, we could cut out now and run,' Jed suggested. 'I got a hunch this job ain't gonna work out like Hogan hoped.'

'Whadja mean?' The Kid turned to him, surprised. 'I ain't backing out now.'

'You shouldn't be mixed up with this mob. They're hardened killers. They go down, it would mean forty years in the slammer at least. You, too. You'd be an old man when you came out. Come on, Kid, let's run. I'm pretty sure this is foolishness.'

'I don't run out on my pals.' The Kid's blue eyes were as sharp as thorns. 'You go if you want to.'

'OK. Don't say I didn't warn you.'

Hogan and his boys rode over the ridge to a point where they could get a view of the railroad from San Francisco winding up the steep slope of the mountain.

'Della, you and Peg Leg take the horses on down the slope a bit. Boys, you get hid in the rocks. Y'all know what to do.'

The excitement was buzzing through the Kid as he found himself a hiding spot beside the track and waited. Minutes passed . . . a quarter of an hour . . . half an hour . . . and, sure enough, there it was, toiling up the slope towards them, the 'Frisco Flyer locomotive, with its cowcatcher, its bell clanging, thrusting black smoke from its tail stack in rhythmic gasps . . . Cha! Cha! Cha! Cha! Behind it were four Pullman coaches and then the Adams Express Car.

A greasy-faced engineer wearing goggles was leaning from the cab. He looked surprised when Hogan ran from the rocks and stepped up on to the footplate, jamming his Remington revolver into his throat. The stoker yelped as Donny did the same from the other side.

'Take it on up as far as the bridge and stop this side,' Hogan yelled, above the racket of the engine.

The train was going at not much

more than a walking pace and the bandits, who had positioned themselves at intervals down the track, jumped aboard the passenger coaches and stormed through firing revolvers and carbines at the ceiling, or at anybody who looked like he might cause trouble, demanding they surrender their valuables. Jed rode along outside, firing into the air, hoping that no passenger would be fool enough to fire back.

'Keep them covered,' Hogan shouted to Donny, jumping from the engine and waiting for the armoured car, with its grilled ironwork across the door and windows, to reach him. He had timed it just right and the wagon came to halt by his side. 'Cut it free.'

Cherokee had brought an axe and he smashed it through a rubber pipe joined to the wagon. Hogan signalled for the engine to back up a bit and it did so as Cherokee knocked the car's coupling free.

'Right!' Hogan signalled to Donny. 'Tell him to take them right across the canyon out of our way.'

As the locomotive and coaches rumbled and rattled slowly away across the rickety bridge to come to a halt on the far side, Hogan looked up at the slit in the door of the armoured car. 'Throw your weapons out and open up,' he yelled, ''less you wanna be blown to Kingdom Come.'

Conductor Flanagan's face appeared at the slit. 'I've told the bank guard here to do as you say, that we ain't got a hell's chance, but he's refusing to see sense.'

The men had dropped from the Pullman coaches, their pockets and gunny sacks stuffed with wallets, watches, rings and necklaces snatched roughly from the pockets and throats of rich men and lady passengers. The Kid had taken one of the bottles from his sack. 'Tell him it only needs a few drops of this stuff and you'll be singing with the angels. It's nitroglycerine. You hear that?'

Those inside obviously had for it was

not long before two revolvers and a carbine were thrust through the slit and the door was unlocked. Flanagan in his uniform stepped out and winked at Hogan, followed by a sullen, bull-necked guard in civilian clothes. Hogan slammed the guard in the jaw with the butt of his revolver, felling him. 'Right, let's see what you got inside, mister.'

'The safe's locked and I don't have a key,' Flanagan said. 'You're going to have to blow it, boys. First, you remember the deal we got, don't you?'

'Sure we remember,' Hogan said. 'You'll get what's coming to you.'

'Stand aside,' the Kid yelled. 'I'll soon fix the dumb safe.'

'Take it easy, Kid,' Hogan warned. 'You don't need much of that stuff — '

But the Kid was already inside the armoured car. He kneeled down and carefully placed his three bottles in front of the big old iron safe. He returned to the door and drawled, 'If I was y'all I'd be taking cover in them rocks.' He pulled out his Allen and

Hopkins, twirled it on his finger, as the men scattered. He jumped down on to the track, peered through the door and took aim. He gritted his teeth, and fired.

Ka-pow! In one blinding flash the heavily built armoured van went up. *Whoompf!* The air waves of the explosion hit the Kid, hurling him off his feet and into the air. As debris was scattered all about them the remains of the safe thumped down into the ground, missing Hogan by a fraction, its door removed, but empty of its contents. Hogan gulped, and put up a hairy arm to protect himself from the falling fragments.

Like a cloud of locusts, bits and pieces of dollar bills were fluttering through the air, blowing away on the mountain breeze.

'There goes our cash!' he bellowed.

The bandits raced after it, trying to snatch at fluttering bills as they fell, scrambling and stooping and jumping away through the rocks. At that height the breeze was fierce and thousands of greenbacks went wafting away down into the canyon. Open-mouthed, Hogan watched his prize disappear before his eyes.

'You durn, lard-brained young fool,' he yelled at the Kid, who was picking himself up, looking somewhat dazed, his clothes in tatters. 'Look what you done.'

'Hey!' The Kid caught a large greenback that drifted down like an autumn leaf. 'Am I concussed, or does this say ten thousand dollars?'

'Give it to me.' Hogan snatched it from him. 'You're right. It does. Well, diddlely-doo. I'll be a bullfrog's granny. I never knew they had notes that big. You think it's real?'

'Course it's real. Look, there's the president's picture. The chief cashier's signature. He wouldn't sign it if it weren't real.'

'But how,' Hogan gulped. 'Where . . . when . . . who would want a note that big?'

'Aw, some big business someplace, I guess. More to the point, how we gonna cash it?'

Stumpy Hogan shook his leonine head, puzzled, and tucked the note into a pocket. 'Let's see what else we can salvage.'

'Hey,' Flanagan whined. 'How about my share?'

'Brother,' Hogan said, 'if you can find it among them rocks you're welcome to it.'

When the gang had hopped about picking up what more they could find, all alas in smaller denomination notes, they returned to the edge of the canyon and were debating whether to climb down its steep sides and search the bottom, when Cherokee yelled a warning. 'Look, there's some other train arriving.'

Many of the people in the passenger coaches had jumped down to see what was going on on the other side of the bridge, pointing to the bandits hopping and skipping about after fluttering notes. Their own engine was idling, but now another little locomotive had come chuffing up from the direction of Cheyenne, huffing and puffing as it eased in on the single track at the far end of *The Flyer*.

'Look at that,' Cherokee yelled, as the side of its goods wagon was let down, and fine-fettle horses were being unloaded. 'It's Remington men!'

'I'll soon stop their game.' The Kid found his carbine and bounded down the rocks to where he had a good view of the bridge. He gritted his teeth, aimed at the first bottle, and squeezed out a slug. Again there was a magnificent roar, a booming, billowing orange flame, and the hundreds of lodge-pole pines that formed the bridge-scaffolding collapsed as if in slow motion, struts and rails hurtling through the air. There was a secondary roar as a bottle exploded at the bottom of the canyon, but the Kid was too busy protecting his head from falling flotsam, so he could not tell if the third bottle had gone up.

When he looked up, oddly enough, the furthest section of the structure was still standing, the rail hanging crazily over its edge. The lawmen in their suits and Stetson had led their horses to the brink to see what was going on, and were pulling high-powered rifles from their saddle boots.

The Kid didn't wait for them to start shooting. He snapped off a shot at where his third bottle should be. The *whoompf* of the explosion shattered the remains of the scaffolding, the blast knocking the detectives of the 'super posse', and their horses, clean off their feet. As the cliff crumbled, three of them and their horses sailed down to plunge into the gorge below.

The Kid cheered and brandished his carbine, hurrying back to join the rest of the gang who were beating a retreat down the track. So much for the Remington boys, he grinned.

Although the safe had been blown through the roof, the armoured car was constructed so solidly that the wheels and bed, with remnants of the walls, still remained intact.

'Let's see if anything's left inside,' Hogan roared.

He led the Kid, Cherokee, Deaf Charley, and Conductor Flanagan, scrambling inside. There were signed notes on the floor and some mailbags still intact. 'There might be valuables in these,' Hogan said, and they began ripping them apart.

They were so intent on their work that they did not notice that the wagon bed of the armoured car had started moving back down the slope, slowly gaining momentum. By the time Hogan looked up they were going at quite a lick.

'Put the damn brake on,' he shouted at the conductor.

'How can I? You axed the air brake.'

'What?' Hogan grabbed at the remains of a wall as the wagon lurched around a bend and threw them all to one side. They hung on to each other or to whatever they could and saw harsh rocks flashing by on either side. They were going at such speed that it would be suicide now to jump. 'This thing's out of control!' Hogan yelped, and there was a note of fear in his voice. 'We're going to crash.'

They glimpsed Della and Peg Leg with the horses waiting for them in a small clearing and gazing after them with looks of amazement on their faces as the former armoured car went hurtling on down the mountainside.

They were travelling at twice the speed of the fastest racehorse, speed they had never known before, fifty, sixty, maybe seventy miles an hour, careering wildly down the curving track, hanging on grimly, expecting any moment that the wagon would jump the rails and send them smashing and toppling down the mountainside into eternity.

'How we gonna get outa this?' Hogan yelled.

'Hell knows,' the Kid gritted out.

'Where do they think they're going?' Della cried, staring after the van careering down the track.

'This ain't no time to be taking a train ride,' Peg Leg tut-tutted. 'Come on, we better go back and pick up that Laverty feller and t'others.'

On the far side of the canyon Joe Dafoe was picking himself up and hanging on to his horse, which was struggling to its feet. 'They make a good job of thangs once they git started,' he drawled, examining the destroyed bridge. He reached for his Winchester in the saddle boot. 'There's one of 'em over there.'

'Don't shoot.' McIntosh pushed his rifle aside. 'That's Laverty. He's beckoning to us to follow.'

'Yeah, that's gonna be easier said than done. It'll take a couple of hours to git across this canyon. We're already three short. They'll be gone with the wind by then.'

'They've got the luck of the devil,' McIntosh replied, as they saw a 'youth' arrive with spare horses and Jed and Bill Laverty climb up. 'I wonder who that one is.'

'What were you waving to 'em for?' Della asked Bill. 'It looked like you was telling 'em to follow us.'

'No,' Bill grinned, adjusting his bowler. 'I was just telling 'em to go to hell. Ain't that so, Jed?'

Jed shook his head, dumbfounded. 'We're all lucky to be alive with that maniac around.'

The men on the runaway armoured car were still hanging on like grim death, but breathed sighs of relief when it careered down the last stretch of the slope and reached the plain. Gradually its hectic pace slowed and it rolled to a halt.

'Jeez!' Dan Hogan gasped. 'Look at Conductor Flanagan, he's gawn as white as a sheet. Bet he's never been taken for a ride like that.'

'Yeuk,' the Kid said. 'I think he's filled his pants.'

'No.' Little Hogan clambered down

and kissed the sand. 'That's a railroad-man's natural stink.'

The others jumped down to join him and began cackling with glee at being still alive, punching and pushing each other.

'Look what you done to my wagon,' Flanagan whined. 'There must be five thousand dollars' worth of damage.'

'You should see the bridge,' Hogan grinned. 'That will cost another five thousand to repair.'

They all doubled up with laughter as Flanagan complained, 'I thought you had an explosives expert.'

They began punching each other again and Hogan could hardly get his words out for laughing. 'That's the Kid. Finest explosives expert in the West.'

'What's the joke?' Della asked, as she came galloping up with the rest of the gang, leading the spare horses.

'What's the joke?' Hogan gasped. 'This is the joke.' He waved the ten-thousand dollar note at her. 'I was going to give Mr Flanagan his share out of this, but I don't think he'd have enough change.'

'Hey, this ain't fair,' the conductor complained, as Hogan struggled to climb on his horse. 'I only found a couple hundred dollars.'

The boys tried to stifle their laughter. Dan Hogan trying to mount up was always an amusing sight as he took a running jump and slid back down again, but it wasn't wise to let him know it. He had killed a man for less.

Hogan decided to climb on a rock and jump in the saddle that way. 'Too bad,' he said to Flanagan. 'So long, sucker.'

'Bastard bandits!' the conductor cried, as he watched them gallop away. 'I mighta known I couldn't trust 'em.'

13

It was opening night at Turner's new saloon — The Robbers' Roost in Eagle Valley — and drinks were on the house. Word had spread and the former ranch house was packed with rustlers, renegades, fugitives from far and wide getting stuck into the crushskull whiskey. Up on the platform three 'bed-wrigglers', were shrilly singing and prancing as a piano player jangled the ivories to not very harmonious effect. In fact, a most unharmonious one.

'Holy toenails, Matt! Can't we do better than that?' Dan Hogan winced. 'I seen better backsides on cows. An' cows don't bellow so bad.'

'I'm afraid they were all I could rake up.' Matt eyed the four gals: Frenchie Nell, her hair bright flame, rumoured to be a voracious nymphomaniac (well weren't all French girls?), Double-Barrelled Martha, shaped like a barrel but not named for that reason, a skinny kid called Lonesome Annie, prone to bursting into tears for no apparent reason, and Pigeon-toed Sal, a hard-drinking Irish woman, who also acted as bar-keep and bouncer, and could wield a mean wagon spoke. They were kicking up their legs, displaying frilly, if not particularly clean drawers, in their version of the Parisian Can-Can. The evil, decadent, and much-banned Can-Can was a new experience for the rough, unshaven men, who gathered before the stage and gawped up at the girls.

'The boys seem to like them,' Matt said, weakly.

'Look, why don't we give the Kid a coupla thousand to go east to Cheyenne or someplace and get us a real good looker who can sing and dance? He's got a way with wimmin.' Hogan said. 'How about it, Kid? Pay her whatever she asks.'

'Sure,' the Kid smiled. 'I'll leave in the morning.'

'Are you crazy?' Della interrupted. 'We don't need no fancy singer. I can sing.'

'Honey, you ever heard them bull-frogs croaking?' Winnemucca asked. 'Need I say more.'

'You got a damn cheek. My voice ain't so bad.'

'Della, you're not exactly the delicate type,' Warner soothed. 'Dan's right. We need a gal to give this place class.'

'Why should anyone like that want to come to this Godforsaken hole?'

'Money talks,' Hogan grinned, passing a wad of two thousand to the Kid. 'Don't come back without her. We're gonna make this the ritziest joint in Wyoming.'

Hogan and his boys were in a celebratory mood. They had managed to pick up about twenty thousand dollars between them of the cash that had been blown sky high. And the ten-thousand dollar note was pinned proudly on the wall behind the bar. The rest, about twenty thousand, had been scattered far and wide. But, why worry? There were plenty more trains to rob.

Bill Lawson and Jed Long leaned on the edge of the bar and watched the shindig, morosely. 'What we gonna do now?' Jed asked.

'I'm taking Warner out.'

'What?'

'Soon as he goes out to the john in the dark I'm gonna grab him, take him back to Utah to stand trial. He's an old pal of Hogan's, and, if I know Hogan, he'll go after him, try to bust him outa jail.'

'You mean you're going to use him as bait?'

'Yeah, a sprat to catch the wolves.'

'What do I do?'

'You stay with them. Try to keep me informed.'

The clean-shaven young 'outlaw' stared at his friend seriously. 'OK, best of luck, Bill.'

'I figure we'll need it. Things aren't going our way.'

The urbane Matt Turner, noting their glasses empty, strolled along. 'Refill, boys?'

'No.' Jed waved the whiskey away. 'That stuff's too strong for me. You got anything non-alcoholic?'

'So happens I have. Fresh out on the market.' He produced a bottle and poured a dark brown fizzy liquid. 'Coca Cola, they call it. They make it from the cola leaf, you know.'

Bill Lawson took a sip, and spat it out. 'Yeuk! Can't see that ever catching on. Gimme a shot.'

'I gotta take a leak,' Warner said. 'Keep an eye on the bar.'

Laverty glanced around and muttered, 'Here we go. Make sure they see next week's *Salt Lake City News*.' And he slipped out after him.

Out in the dark he saw Warner up against a wall. He stuck his Krug in his back, slipped his revolver from his belt.

'Get up on a horse, Matt. We're

taking a ride. One squeak out of you and you're dead.'

★   ★   ★

The Kid had left before sun-up, with the two thousand in his pocket, unaware that Matt and Bill were missing. He caught the first train east from Rock Springs. He found that the sprawling cattle town of Cheyenne had its own Theatre of Varieties where top of the bill was 'The Scintillating and Exciting Miss Hetty Pace — Straight From Her Success on Broadway'. The Kid duded himself up in a green lovat suit, with velvet collar and cravat. He had a bath, and even cleaned his boots. He took the best seat, a box hanging almost over the stage. He was mightily impressed by the whole fandangle, the orchestra scraping their fiddles in the pit, the packed house of motley people, the gas footlights flaring, and was transported into another world when the curtain went up, jugglers, trick cyclists, sharp-shooters. When Hetty stepped out on to what looked like the deck of a ship at sea, the HMS *Pinafore*, and announced herself to be 'Sweet li'l Buttercup' with a tray of goodies to sell to the crew he was smitten. He had never set eyes on such a divine-looking young lady: she had the face of an alabaster angel! How did she hit those high notes? How did she remember all them witty words?

He could hardly wait for her appearance in the finale, this time as a pirate chief from some place called Penzance. And it was as if she were smiling straight at him, their eyes clashing. 'Yeah,' he roared. 'Bravo!'

He found he was not the only admirer. Down an alley outside the stage door was a queue of Johnnies with posies of flowers in their paws. He snatched one, shoved them protesting aside, and announced to the stage manager that he was there on theatrical business. Hetty was taking off her costume behind a screen when he was shown in, revealing her attractive bare shoulders.

'I don't think I've had the pleasure, Mr . . . '

'Winnemucca. Nope, I ain't had the pleasure of you, neither. You was a knock-out, Hetty. I'm here with an offer you cain't refuse. Four weeks at the Eagle Valley theatre, West Wyoming, at a fee of one thousand dollars. How's that hit ya?'

'I'm not sure I've ever heard of that venue.' Hetty looked somewhat flustered as she quickly finished dressing. 'I'm scheduled to appear at the Opera House, Virginia City.'

'Aw, you can go there any day. We gotta have you, gal. You're the greatest. Let's talk about this over some grub.'

'Grub?'

'Yeah. Chow. There's a high-class joint up the street. I see they got oysters and salmon, elk pie and sweet potatoes on the menu. Let's do it large. I'm flush. We could even have some of that Frenchie Champagne.'

'You know how to tempt a girl, Mr Winnemucca.'

'Call me Kid.'

'I'll join you if you promise this doesn't commit me.' Hetty was in a summer dress of pink candy-stripe, the skirt daringly high above the ankles to give a glimpse of her white stockings and silver slippers. Her straw hat was covered in imitation fruit. 'We can discuss your offer over dinner.'

'Commit you? Naw. This is all above board.'

It was, indeed, a fine meal, and Hetty wished her dress was not quite so wasp-waisted. A bowl of strawberries and cream made a fine conclusion. The blue-eyed Kid was amusing although his 'theatre' sounded to be somewhat out in the wilds. But a thousand dollars was not to be sneezed at. It was treble what she'd been getting at most of these cowtowns. 'If I could have your guarantee of protection. There are some rough characters around these parts. And, it is to be understood, I appear solely as a singer, two performances a day. I have to protect my voice. This cash doesn't include any other services, like being a waitress girl, if you know what I mean.'

'Sure.' The Kid slapped his revolver. 'You got my personal protection. Sing. Thass all you gotta do.'

'Then it's agreed.' She offered her hand. 'When do we leave?'

'When you're ready.' He hung on to her hand and studied her. 'Here.' He took out his wallet and slapped down $250 in greenbacks. 'Thass your first week's salary. To show I ain't joking.'

'Well!' Hetty's eyes widened 'I accept in good faith.'

'How about we catch the train in the mornin' to Rock Springs?' the Kid said, when he walked her back to her boarding-house.

'No. My contract's not concluded here. But I would be able to leave in three days.'

'Great. I'll hang around.'

Hetty gave an indignant gasp when

he coiled an arm around her waist, pulled her to him, and planted a kiss on her lips. She jerked her face away and struggled free.

'No, Kid, I'm sorry. If that's part of the deal, it's not on.' She retreated on to the lighted porch. 'I'm afraid I want no romantic entanglements with anyone.'

'Aw, Hetty,' the Kid frowned. 'It's jest that you're such an angel. You cain't blame me for trying?'

'And an angel is how I intend to stay.'

'OK. If thass how you want it. There'll be no entangling. Just say you'll come, gal.'

* * *

MORMON PREACHER ARRESTED! screamed the headline of the *Salt Lake City News*.

'What in tarnation's goin' on?' Dan Hogan bellowed as he got young Jed Long to read out the item when they visited Rock Springs for supplies.

'Remington detective Joe Dafoe whisked Matt Turner away from under the noses of the Hole-in-the-Wall gang at one of their hide-outs in the Wyoming hills this week. The former preacher is to be arraigned for fraud and homicide. Also arrested in the darkness of a daring night raid, was a bandit known as Butcher Bill Laverty, wanted for rustling, robbery, rape and arson. Both men have been confined in Bear Lake City prison to await trial.'

'Laverty, too? I wondered where them two galoots had gotten to.' Hogan stared at the dots on the page wishing he had learned to read. 'This is a dastardly outrage. We gotta do something about this. They cain't do this to me.'

* * *

'We're gonna need some cash to set up a fighting fund for Matt,' Hogan said, as he and a dozen men crossed the Salt River range and headed towards the

Great Salt Lake. 'How about that bank at Montpelier? It ain't far off.'

'Jasus!' Peg Leg had gone behind a rock to urinate and disturbed a skunk. He pulled out his gun and took a shot at it. 'Aw, hell!' The skunk sprayed him with its foul smell and made a run for freedom. The incensed cripple chased after it, shooting crazily, until he had killed it. He picked it up, sourly, by its pungent tail and growled, 'Varmint!'

'Don't come near us,' Jed shouted. 'Yuk! You stink so much you're scaring my hoss.'

'He allus was a lousy skunk,' Deaf Charley growled. 'Now he smells like one.'

Peg Leg had difficulty getting on his horse, which shied away from his disgusting aroma. The gang galloped ahead keeping well upwind from him. As they trailed in to Montpelier Hogan said, 'I got an idea. We'll send Peg Leg in. He'll be our secret weapon.' He nearly retched as Peg Leg drew near, he was so nauseating. He pulled up his bandanna and pointed, 'Go take it.'

'I gotta git a change of clothes and have a bath,' Peg Leg whined, as he pulled out his long-barrelled revolver, and glanced about the semi-deserted main street. 'I cain't stand the stink of myself.'

The boys near collapsed with laughter as, after a few seconds, a bearded Mormon and three of his wives came stumbling out, gagging into their handkerchiefs, quickly followed by the banker himself.

'Peg Leg sure knows how to clear a bank,' Della yelled.

Peg Leg ran out stuffing dollars into the capacious pockets of his old cavalry coat. 'I never seen a banker so eager to give away his money,' he shouted, struggling to get in the saddle as his horse reared and kicked, shying away from his scent. 'Wait for me, boys,' he cried plaintively as they galloped away. 'It ain't my fault. The damn skunk was too fast on the draw. He got his shot in first.'

When they got to Bear River City the first thing they did was go to the bath-house and buy themselves clean clothes. They felt better for that, but a faint aroma still clung to the dollar notes as Hogan counted Peg Leg's haul. 'Another two thousand for the fighting fund.'

'You're crazy,' Donny told him. 'We'll never get him out of that jailhouse. It's built like Fort Knox and they've brought in extra guards. Matt's being a former preacher has given his case special interest. The news sheets are full of it. They're already talking about a plot to get him out.'

'Money talks,' Dan said. 'You'd be surprised. You boys wait here. I got people to see.'

It was the Fourth of July and the town was in a riot of celebration. Folks were singing and dancing in the streets as fireworks whooshed into the sky, and some fellow had got hold of a horseless carriage, a Benz Victoria, built in '93, like two armchairs on wheels, with resplendent red-leather upholstery and cream paintwork. He was driving around the streets, parping an ornate snake-horn, pursued by children running after it, or hanging on the back.

Lawyer Strauss was locking up his office. He peered over wire spectacles. 'Can I help you?'

'No, but you can help Matt Turner when his case comes up.' Hogan slapped a wad of notes into his hand. 'That's a thousand, just for starters.'

Strauss eyed him sharply. 'Who are you?'

'That don't matter. What matters is you git Matt out. If you don't we're gonna git annoyed.'

'You'd better come in.' Strauss quickly slipped the cash in a drawer. 'I'll do my best, but it's not going to be easy. They've got a new machine called the electric chair and they're eager to try it out. Turner's up for homicide. I can't give any guarantees.'

'So, what else can I do for my pal?'

'It might be best if you went to see

the judge.' Strauss scribbled down a name and address. He picked up his telephone machine's hearing-piece, wound the battery, and spoke into the mouthpiece. 'Judge, I'm sending a friend over to see you. He's a very generous man. It's about the Matt Turner case. Maybe we can help him?'

Judge Plymouth had a big house on the edge of town. Hogan hammered with his revolver butt on the front door. A flunkey invited him in. Out the window he could see a silver-haired man with his family, probably grandchildren, having some fireworks festivities of their own. Judge Plymouth came in and beckoned him to his study.

'I'll be needing two thousand for expenses,' were his first words.

'You're some greedy bastard, aincha? What is this, some kinda squeeze?' But Hogan dug deep and hauled out more wads of notes. 'What do I get for this?'

'Turner's trial is pending and I will be presiding. I've already sworn in the jury members. You can have their names and a list of witnesses. You might like to put a bit of pressure on them.' The judge was busy tucking the cash away in his safe. He produced a list of names. 'This here's the jury. But I'm not sure that tampering will be necessary. I'm sure Mr Strauss and I can get Turner off on some technicality or other.'

'You'd better, mister. And this other fella, Laverty. He ain't a personal pal of mine, like Matt. But we want him out, too. For the same cash. No more. That's it.'

The judge glanced at the coarse-featured, hairy little man who had climbed up on to a chair opposite him. He was so stumpy his feet didn't touch the carpet. The judge couldn't help smiling. He looked like some dirty Neanderthal.

'I don't like grinners,' Hogan growled. 'If it's my verticality amuses you I should warn you, I've slit men's throats for less.'

'No, no, not at all,' the judge

protested. 'Glad to do business with you, Mr . . . er . . . well, never mind. Now, if you'll excuse me, I have family duties. Happy Independence Day to you.'

'Yeah, same to you. Gran'kids, eh? Right, I'll remember where you live. The syndicate don't like to be double-crossed. If you try anything, I'll be back. Get me? We don't give a damn who you are.'

He returned to town and pushed through the throng of the saloon, where everyone was getting rousingly drunk.

'Phew!' he said. 'That judge! I sometimes think I'm in the wrong profession.' He stared at his boys, morosely. 'What's the world coming to? Bribery and corruption. Machines like that Benz that might well replace the horse. Wire going up everywhere. They even got machines that fly, so I hear. If the posse git hold of them what chance will we have of hidin' out in the hills?'

'*Si*, it look like the sun is setting on the days of the free-riding cowboy,' Joe

196

agreed, and the others nodded, dolefully.

'Jed, you copy out these names and addresses. Give a couple to each of the boys. You gotta make some calls on the jury. Don't git too heavy. Jest warn 'em it'll be in everybody's best interests if Matt and Bill git off.'

The gang, Texican Joe, Tom O'Leary, Muddy Waters, Mad Dog, Peg Leg, Deaf Charley Sparrow, Cherokee Williams, and the others, shuffled off to do Hogan's bidding.

'Hech!' Hogan spat tobacco juice at the floorboards, and said to Della and Donny. 'I need a drink after that. It's a dirty ol' world.'

Jed slipped away on pretext of seeing to the jury. At the telegraph office he composed a cable and sent it to Detective McIntosh at Cheyenne. 'Maybe it's time I got out, too,' he muttered to himself. But, reluctantly, he returned to the saloon.

14

Three days of living high on the hog in Cheyenne had left the Kid feeling a tad jaded. He hadn't got anywhere personally with Hetty but she had promised to take up his offer. Today was the big day. She had promised to meet him at the railroad station.

When the westbound locomotive from Chicago pulled into Cheyenne at nine in the morning the Kid noticed that the Adams Express car at the back had its door solidly barred, but a small window high up on its side appeared to be just glass, and it was positioned beneath one of the knob-like air vents on the roof. Winnemucca watched a uniformed guard lock himself inside. He had a quarter of an hour while the locomotive took on wood and water, so he slipped back across the street to a store which sold working-clothes and equipment for railroad men. He quickly purchased a navy-blue boiler suit, or coverall, a large suitcase, a canvas haversack, and a woollen balaclava, with holes for eyes and mouth, which train drivers donned when they were hurtling across the Rockies in a blizzard and had to peer out from the cab. The Kid had had a bright idea.

'Where is that gal? Has she changed her mind?'

No, a horsecab came clopping up and Hetty waved. She had tossed and turned all night, serious doubts in her mind, but had decided to take a chance. The Kid helped her with her small wooden trunk, they climbed aboard and found a seat in the restaurant car as the bell clanged and the locomotive began to pull out.

'We're on our way, Hetty. How about some breakfast?'

He raised a finger to a coloured waiter in a white coat and ordered ham and eggs and coffee. The waiter was very attentive because the Kid in his natty velvet-collared coat and cravat, and Hetty in an outfit of dove grey, with a hat and travelling cloak to match, looked like a wealthy young couple who might leave a big tip.

'Might I ask why you're carrying an empty suitcase?'

'It's for you, darlin',' he said, lifting it on top of the trunk. 'We might need to buy you a couple more outfits. Why don't you slap one of them fancy labels of yours on?'

There were not many travellers in the Pullman restaurant car and, after breakfasting, the Kid sprawled out on the luxurious padded seat, lit a cheroot, and watched the prairie roll by.

On they rattled through the morning, stopping at Medicine Bow and Rawlins, then on again. The Kid seemed to be preoccupied. When the conductor came through calling out that in half an hour they would be in Bitter Creek, he got up, taking his canvas bag, and said he was going to stretch his legs.

Winnemucca strolled back through

the more crowded second class carriages until he reached the viewing platform and the 'bridge' linking them to the Adams armoured car. Yes, the door was solidly barred. No way in there. He glanced back. There was no one around. He pulled the coverall over his suit, and the balaclava over his head. He stuffed the canvas bag in his pocket, and nimbly climbed to the roof of the car. Crouched on its rocking and rolling top he edged forward to the knoblike air vent. He took a rawhide cord from his pocket and tied it tight round the vent. The wind rattled through his clothing as the train thundered along at top speed. Suddenly he heard a long drawn out *Whooooo-whaaaaaaa* . . . of the engine's steam whistle and, looking ahead at its tall stack pumping woodsmoke, and the carriages bumping along behind it, he saw a tunnel looming up. The Kid flattened himself as they rushed into the dark hole, smoke and cinders almost choking him. Fortunately it was not a long tunnel and they were quickly through.

'Now!' Winnemucca swung wildly out over the edge, clinging to the cord, and for moments was out of control, hanging in space, wondering desperately if he could hold on. The cord was cutting into his fingers. One slip and he would be flung tumbling under the churning wheels below. *Whooo . . . whaaaaa . . . .* Oh, no! Another tunnel heaving into sight.. It was now or never!

The Kid braced his boots against the side of the van, kicked himself out, and swung back in, boots first, smashing through the side window of the van.

'What the devil?' The uniformed guard spun around, staring at him as if he were Satan himself, sprung from the nether world. 'Where the hell?' He looked around to reach for his carbine.

Too late. The Kid scrambled up, pulling the Hopkins .36 from his pocket. 'Don't ask no questions, mister. Just open the lock of that safe.'

'Are you Oliver Perry?' The name of

a young Wyoming robber renowned for his daring and violence came into the guard's mind.

'Yeah, that's me.' The Kid clouted him across the jaw with his left fist. 'You'll hurry it up if you wanna reach the end of this line. I'll give you to the count of three.'

At two the guard decided discretion was better than valour and opened the tumbler-lock of the safe. 'There it is, forty thousand dollars' worth of jewellery. How did you know?'

'I didn't.' The Kid gulped with surprise as he opened one of the packets — full of diamond rings, bracelets, brooches. 'Gee, thanks, mister. Much obliged.' He buffaloed him across the back of his neck with the butt of the Hopkins. 'Sorry about that.'

The Kid pulled off his mask and coverall. He loaded the packets into his canvas bag, took the keys from the belt of the unconscious guard, unlocked the car, stepped out, relocked it, tossed the keys, his boiler suit and balaclava away into the passing weeds and, pausing only to comb fingers through his hair and brush down his suit, returned to the restaurant car.

'Any more of that coffee?' he asked, as he sat down beside Hetty.

She poured him a cup from the silver pot. 'What kept you?'

'Just taking a little air.'

'Hold still.' She took a dainty handkerchief from her sleeve. 'You've got black grits on your face.' She dabbed them off.

'Thanks. Dirty old things these trains.'

They were pulling into the lonesome stop of Bitter Creek out on the prairie. There was a sudden hullabaloo. The guard had come to and was shouting out of the window of the Adams car. The town sheriff and his deputy were summoned. They came running. Folks were hanging out of the windows to see what was going on. While they did so, the Kid, unnoticed, slipped the canvas bag and its contents into the empty suitcase and locked it.

'They're saying something about a robbery,' Hetty said, looking back from the window.

'Really?' The Kid sipped his coffee and lit another cheroot. 'Sure hope we ain't gonna be delayed.'

The town law officers, the conductor, and shaken-looking guard were coming along through the carriages, giving anybody with a canvas bag, which was almost everybody, a once-over.

'Siddown,' the Kid said, putting an arm around Hetty's waist and pulling her down to sit on his lap. 'Relax.'

Hetty gave a squeal of surprise and struggled to be free, but he held her tight close, smiling into her eyes.

'I don't know what you got against me.' He put his hand behnd her nape, and before she could resist, kissed her.

The lawmen and conductor glanced at the wealthy-looking young couple. 'Must be on honeymoon,' the Adams guard said, and they passed by.

Hetty regained her seat and her

equilibrium, pushing the Kid away. 'I've told you,' she hissed. 'If you try that again the deal's off. In fact, I'm having serious second thoughts.'

'OK, it's just that you're such a honey, I can't resist. All right, no more' — he watched the men go on down the train — 'I git the message. I'll behave.'

'It's not that I don't like you. In fact, I'm flattered. You're a handsome young rogue. But you must see my position, I can't go around making love to every — '

'You're a lady and me — I ain't a gent.'

'What's happening?' a woman was asking.

'It's that Oliver Perry. He's struck again,' the Kid said.

The lawmen were crunching back along the track. 'There's no sign of him,' one shouted. 'We reckon he musta jumped off straight away back a few miles. We'll get a posse and hounds and go after him.'

Eventually the express pulled away

and the Kid smiled, 'Them corn-sucking hicks will never catch him. He's too good for 'em.'

As the train rattled on its way, next stop Rock Springs, Hetty studied him with her serious eyes.

'What do you do when you're not arranging concerts?'

'I represent The Wyoming Syndicate. High Finance. We juggle funds. Take 'em from one account, put 'em in another. We're not all hopeless saddle-bums out here, ya know.'

'Really, like a stockbroker?'

'Yeah, you got it.' He grinned at her, not certain what a stockbroker was. 'Used to deal in cattle. Now I deal in cash.'

* * *

'Here we are, sweetheart!' The Kid stepped from the train at Rock Springs and handed Hetty down. 'You hang on here while I go along to the livery and hire a buggy.'

When the train pulled away Hetty was left standing by the track beneath the water tower in the blazing heat. It suddenly seemed very quiet and lonesome. She looked across a dirt street at a row of dilapidated false fronts, mustangs at a hitching rail patiently bearing their fate, the tormenting flies. Some scruffy men tumbled out of the batwing doors of a saloon and stood in the shade of the canopy staring across at her. One muttered something and gave a coarse laugh. She ignored them, beginning to wish she had never come.

'Hi!' The Kid came along in a light, high-wheeled buggy. 'Jump aboard.' He roped her trunk and the suitcase on the back, climbed back on the buckboard, gave a flick of the reins and they were away. Out they went at a fast clip into the vastness of the prairie.

Hetty, although billed as 'a Broadway star', had, in fact, only been in the chorus of HMS *Pinafore*. She had a pleasant voice, but it had limitations. It was to get out of the chorus line that she had devised the tour. She wanted to put some cash in the bank, make her name, but the travelling, the small towns, were proving tedious and tawdry. And she had the gnawing feeling that this time she had made a big mistake.

'We're not likely to be robbed, are we? I didn't like the look of those men.'

'Nah! Us Westerners are gen'lemen. We got great respect for a lady. We don't see many.'

'I don't know why I feel so uneasy,' she said, more to herself. 'I've been in one shooting incident on this tour. I mean, that's a once-in-a-lifetime thing. The odds are surely against me being involved in another.'

'A shoot-out? Where?'

'Belle Fourche. A girl was killed.'

He frowned. 'Yeah, I heard. So you were there?'

'Yes, I was on the stage. I only knew her a couple of hours. I felt sorry for her poor husband.'

'What happened to him?'

'I' — she glanced at him — 'I don't know.'

They fell silent as they drove for hours across the most bare and desolate countryside Hetty had ever seen, bouncing and rattling through rutted gorges. She was too busy hanging on to her seat to talk. At one point, on a precipitous canyonside, she was sure they were going to tip over, but the Kid yelled at the horse and they went rushing down to hit rock bottom.

'Where on earth are we going?' she cried. 'It's like the end of the world.'

As the sun began to sink over the horizon in streamers of crimson cloud she saw the ancient ranch house, built of clapboard, stark and alone.

'Here we are, the Eagle Valley Concert House. It ain't quite like the Palace, but it's home.'

Hetty swallowed her dismay as they drew in outside the dilapidated building. On a board over the door, in crude red-paint letters, was scrawled, THE ROBBERS' ROOST. She met the gaze of a fat floozy hanging from an upstairs window, who giggled, 'Hi, Kid. You got us some new gal power?'

'Is this where I am to appear?' Hetty asked, startled.

'Yeah, come in and meet the boys and gals.' He grabbed hold of her in his arms, jumping lightly up to the veranda, kicking open the front door. 'Hey, y'all. Meet your new singing lady. All the way from Cheyenne to entertain us. Miss Hetty Pace.'

Lonesome Annie and Frenchie Nell were sprawled on a horsehair sofa, and looked up lethargically. Pigeon-toed Sal was behind the bar and had her usual hard face. The piano player, a seedy individual called Costain, badly in need of a clean shirt and a shave, did not seem over-impressed. 'You mean she's gonna be the new canary?'

'Yeah, so where is everybody? Where's Matt? Where's Dan?'

'Matt's in jail,' Sal scowled. 'They gone to bust him out.'

The Kid put a finger to his lips. 'No

need to go into that just yet. How about a drink? What's it to be, Hetty?'

'You wouldn't have a glass of champagne? I have to be careful of my throat.'

'Rum and whiskey's all we got,' Sal said, sourly.

'Try one of them Colas,' the Kid said. 'The latest thang.'

'Have you any ice?'

'Hech!' Frenchie Nell scoffed. 'Where you think this is? Delmonico's?'

Hetty sipped at the drink, looking about her uneasily. 'There don't seem to be many customers.'

'Aw, it'll liven up once the boys git back. I'll show you to your room.'

'I'd love a hot bath.'

'Hech!' Sal screeched. 'A hot bath! In this heat? There's the pump out back. Cold water's good enough for us other gals. Go give her a scrub, Kid. A splash of my French perfume and she'll have the boys linin' up to service her. Only trouble is she's gonna be takin' business from us.'

'That's enough, Sal. Hetty's here solely as a singer. That's what Dan said. I given her my word. She ain't a two-bit whore. She's been on Broadway.'

'You mean to say she ain't gonna be dropping her drawers?' Double Barrel Martha drawled as she leaned over the balcony outside the upstairs rooms. 'How much they payin' her?'

'Two-fifty a week I'm entitled to. That's the spoken contract.' Hetty bridled up, indignantly. 'For two concerts a day. But I think I've made a mistake. I'd be obliged if you would take me back to Rock Springs in the morning, Kid.'

'I cain't do that, honey,' the Kid protested. 'A contract's a contract.'

'Good ol' Winnemucca,' Double Barrel cried. 'Ain't he the kidder? Champagne, hot baths, no horizontal work, fer two-fifty a week? Thass crazy.'

'It sure is,' Costain said. 'An' there's nobody to damn well sing to, anyway.'

'Quit it,' the Kid shouted. 'I say what goes while Dan's away. Come on,

Hetty. Let's find you a room.'

He took her elbow and led her up the stairs as Pigeon-toed Sal shouted, 'The stuck-up li'l bitch'll do what she's told. I'm in charge of the gals in this house, Kid, not you.'

Double Barrel blocked their way at the head of the stairs, chewing on Mexican gum in her trollopy way. 'Look at Li'l Miss Goody Two Shoes.' She flicked her hand, knocking Hetty's hat back. 'She thinks all she gotta do is sing.'

'Get out of my way.' In sudden fierceness, the delicate-looking girl smashed her handbag into her. 'You — you slut.'

Double Barrel staggered back. 'Get *her*!' she cooed, fear mingled with awe in her eyes.

'What have you brought me to? Some brothel at the back of beyond? How dare you?' Hetty slammed the bedroom door, and paced up and down. She was almost in tears. 'How could you?'

'They ain't so bad. It's jest their fun.

You'll soon git used to us.'

'I sincerely hope not. Oh my God!' she pointed at the rumpled sheets on a stained, striped mattress. 'You don't expect me to sleep on that? It's probably crawling.'

'It's only stains. Just the boys. I'll scrape it off.'

'Scrape it off? Haven't you any clean sheets? Do you really expect me to stay in this filthy hole? I want to leave, tomorrow, first thing.'

'Cain't be done, honey. Hey, look, I'll go light the stove, bile up some water fer ya bath. I'l ask Sal about the sheets.'

Hetty was standing by the window, her hand to her brow, trying to prevent herself from breaking down into sobbing.

'I'll go git the luggage.' said the Kid.

He returned with her trunk and the canvas bag. He took out a necklace, held it up to the light. 'Look what I got ya. It'll look great around your slim throat. It's real diamonds.'

Hetty's eyelashes fluttered as she

examined the necklace and watched the Kid tip out rings, watches, bracelets in silver, gold and pearl, onto the bed.

'It's worth a fortune,' he gloated.

'Oh, no!' She tossed the necklace away as if it might contaminate her. 'It was you! Wasn't it? Oh, my God! What a fool I am!'

'Hell, baby, what's wrong with you? This is good stuff. What was theirs is now ours. It's simple as that.'

'And I suppose that money you paid me. That was all stolen too?'

The Kid shrugged and grinned. 'It's genuine cash. It ain't counterfeit. Nuthin' wrong with it.'

Hetty sighed, and stared at him. 'You've brought me to a den of thieves and whores and you really expect me to stay here?'

The Kid's dark face hardened. 'Honey, you got no choice.'

15

There was a hue and cry in Bear River City. Matt Turner's trial was due to start the next day, but members of the Hole-in-the-Wall gang had been spotted in the town. It was rumoured they would try to get him out of prison by force of arms. Hogan decided there was nothing for it but to show their heels. He and the boys hid out in Bear Canyon, high against a cliff wall, about ten miles out. He had to reconsider his plan of campaign.

They were crouched around a fire cooking up some breakfast when Waters yelled, 'Rider comin'!'

It was Tom O'Leary and he was riding hard. He had to jump from his bronc and lead it as he climbed up to them where they were huddled on the shelf of a shallow cave. He was waving a newspaper in his hand. 'They're on to us,' he gasped out. 'That super posse's arrived. I seen 'em, Joe Dafoe and the others unloading their horses from the train.'

MOST DESPERATE PLOT UNEARTHED! proclaimed the banner headline of the *Bear River Citizen*, with the sub-heads, 'Hole-in-the-Wall gang propose to liberate their pal!' 'They looted banks to get defence cash'. 'Judge accused of corruption'.

The report stated:

Startling and sensational revelations show that the gang who committed the recent bank robbery at Montpelier did so in order to get the cash to bribe leading members of the judiciary. They have also threatened to kill anyone who takes the stand to testify against Turner, who is due to start trial tomorrow.'

Another cross-head stated,

Clever Work of Detectives

Remington agency detectives raided the home of respectable citizen, Judge Plymouth, and found thousands of dollars in notes in his possession with the same serial numbers as those of the stolen money. He has been arrested and charged with accepting a bribe, although he protests his innocence.

The well-known lawyer, Mr Strauss, was also raided and found to have one thousand dollars of stolen cash in his possession. He claims, however, that the money was paid to him as a retainer by an unknown visitor to his office, who hired him to defend Turner. He claims he was unaware it was stolen and acted legitimately.

The story was splattered all over the front page with photographs of Matt Turner, Dan Hogan and various gang members.

Another shrieking headline proclaimed: MAY BE A BATTLE! and announced:

The Inter-state Super-Posse has arrived in town. It is understood the bandits are now camped in Bear Canyon ten miles out of town. The officers are preparing to go into the mountains this morning and a bloody conflict is looked for. Any able-bodied man who is prepared to ride with the posse should report, with his own rifle and horse, to the law officers immediately.'

'Whoo!' Joe Pizanthia gave a whistle of awe. 'How the hell did they find all this out? Looks like we've lost the chance of getting Matt out, boys. We'd better git outa here.'

'Too late,' Deaf Charley shouted, pointing to a distant chasm where a large body of horsemen could be seen churning through a pocket of sand.

'Here they come.'

'We can take 'em,' Mad Dog Harry cried, and rested his rifle on a rock. 'What you ninnies scared of?' He clacked the bolt of his heavy old English Enfield .303 and sent a bullet whining towards the oncoming horsemen.

Della bit her scarred lip. 'Those super-posse boys aren't novices. They know how to shoot. It looks like they've got a good backing of townsmen.'

'They'll make mincemeat of us.' There was a note of panic in Muddy Waters' voice. 'I say we surrender.'

Mad Dog smashed his rifle barrel across his neck, felling him. 'Next man says that gets the same. C'mon. Start shooting.'

The other dozen men jumped to join him, levering slugs into carbines and rifles, sending a fusillade of lead down into Bear Canyon. But the posse was out of range, splitting into two groups as if to encircle them, and coming steadily on.

'I dunno,' Hogan growled, his instinct of self-preservation overcoming his anger. 'Maybe Della's right. Maybe we should split up? Cherokee and you, Peg Leg, head south for the Canyonlands. Take four of the boys. Deaf Charley, you and Muddy and Tom git back to the Hole. Joe, Della, Jed, me and Donny will ride for Eagle Valley. Get goin', Cherokee, my ol' pal, we'll cover you.'

The pure-blood Indian, in his dark suit and high-bowled hat, did not argue with Hogan. He leaped lightly on to his horse, and set off at a gallop along the ridge, followed by Peg Leg, and four others. There was a shout from the men down below, one pointing at the skyline. The posse came to a halt as Hogan and his men loosed a hail of lead at them. They scrambled for cover and took up firing positions. Joe Dafoe had his telescopic sights on Cherokee half a mile away. He squeezed out a shot and the Indian went tumbling from his bronc, slithering down the shale of the cliffside to lie inert. Dafoe cursed as Peg Leg disappeared over the skyline, but he managed to take out three more of the fleeing men.

His five super-posse members were taking beads with their powerful rifles on the rest of the gang, who were hauling themselves up into their saddles. 'They're making a run for it,' Dafoe shouted. 'Give 'em all you got.'

Pow! A slug thudded into Muddy Waters' back, and he threw his hands up in agony, tumbling to the rocks. *Pa-dang*! Another whistled an inch past Hogan's head as he quirted his bronc up the canyon. *Pa-zoom*! Tom O'Leary leapt like a scalded cat as a .357 manstopper ripped through him. Other of the outlaws were falling like ninepins as they tried to make their escape.

'What you waitin' for?' Donny howled at Jed, aiming his revolver at him. 'You're ridin' with us, mister.'

Jed shrugged and climbed on his horse as bullets whistled about them. He put spurs to its sides and hurried after Della and Dan.

'How about you, Mad Dog?' Donny yelled. 'You gonna face 'em all on your own?'

'No way,' Holm grinned, dodging over towards his horse. 'I'm coming with you.'

When they reached the rim of the canyon they sent some farewell shots down at the posse, and went racing away. Soon they would be into a maze of rocky canyons that the Hogans knew like each other's ugly faces. It would be easy enough to throw off pursuit. When they paused for a breather Della asked, 'What about Matt?'

'Matt's had it,' Hogan growled, his face grim. 'He'll fry. Somebody's gonna pay.'

★ ★ ★

Gunshots, a yip-yipping and yee-hooing, the sound of pounding hooves roused Hetty from her sleep. She had remained in her baking hot room all day, afraid to go down. The Kid had brought her coffee and biscuits, and been cheerfully attentive, but made it clear she was their prisoner. She dreaded the thought of what was in store for her. She peered from the window and saw seven riders galloping towards the saloon, milling their mustangs in a cloud of dust, firing off revolvers into the air, shouting out to each other and the gals on the veranda, jumping from their saddles and pushing into The Robbers' Roost. She listened to them clamouring and stomping noisily along the bar below, and whispered to herself, 'Oh, my God, why did I ever come to this horrible place? They must be the ones who murdered Cassie.'

Down in the bar Dan Hogan was pumping the Kid's hand, slapping his back, and filling him in on how once more they had escaped the so-called Super-Posse, and on what had occurred. 'So where's that new gal we paid fer? Let's be taking a peep. Sal says she's a li'l cracker.'

'There's a problem,' the Kid frowned. 'She's restin' right now. She's a li'l upset. She won't perform. She wants to go back to Rock Springs.'

'What?' Hogan roared, slapping the Kid on the back of his neck with his massive hand. 'What's the matter with you, boy? You paid her, aincha? So, you tell her we're waiting to see her dance and sing. That's what she's here for. We've had a long ride. We need to unwind. Come on, Sal, where's the liquor? One glassful ain't no good to me.'

'You don't understand, Dan. She's a classy gal. She was expecting better than this.'

'Better? What could be better than The Robbers' Roost sporting-house and two-fifty a week? What's she got to be upset about? Tell her to get damn well started.'

The Kid shrugged, signalled Costain to get on his piano stool — they had been practising the piece all day, trying to tempt Hetty down.

'Come on, honey,' he said, bursting into her room. 'Give us one rip-roaring performance tonight and I promise tomorrow you can go.' He went to her trunk. 'Here's ya Li'l Miss Buttercup costume. Come on, put it on.'

'You give your word?'

'Yeah, sure. I'll help ya out. I'll sing along. Look, do me a favour, the boys, they were lookin' forward to this. We been through a bad time.'

'All right,' she said. 'One perfor-mance tonight.'

Down below, the Knock 'em Dead home-brew whiskey was having its effect. Hogan and Joe Pizanthia were bemoaning their bad luck. Mad Dog and Donny were bitterly berating each other.

'It's his fault,' Donny shouted, pointing at Jed. 'Someone's been feedin' 'em information and I'm pretty sure it's him.'

Jed went for his .32 revolver but Donny was too fast for him, knocking it from his hand and sending it clattering across the floor. Mad Dog's fist smashd into his gut, doubling him up, and he was hurled against the bar.

'Wait a minute,' Donny spat out. 'Don't kill him, just yet. I want to find out who this greenhorn is, who he's working for. Then I'll kill him slowly, bone by bone. Tie him to that chair.'

'Ta-ran-ta-ra!' The Winnemucca Kid, cutting a flash in his new suit, diamond stickpin in his cravat, burst out on to the landing. 'Lade-eees and Gen'lmen, allow me to present, straight from her smash-hit role on Broadway, Noo York, the scintillattin', the exotic, the lovely Miss Hetty Pace.'

Hetty appeared behind him in her Buttercup outfit, low-slung blouse and skirt split to show a fine pair of stockinged legs in silver high heels, a false showgirl's smile on her painted lips hiding her fear.

'I *am* the Captain of the *Pinafore*', Winnemucca crooned, dancing down the stairs, twirling a gold-knobbed cane, as Hetty followed him and Costain started jangling the ivories.

'Hey,' Dan Hogan roared. 'We paid to hear her not you.'

'Here she is.' The Kid picked Hetty up, whirled her around, and planted her on the stage. 'Go on, Het.'

A 'show must go on' instinct made Hetty burst into song. The rough men and girls were just a haze to her. She began tossing goodies from her tray, 'I've toffee and jacky and all kinds of baccy . . . '

Her singing brought the house down, as they say. The men roared for an encore. Suddenly through the canopy of tobacco fumes Hetty saw Jed Long, blood trickling from his mouth, tied to a chair in a corner of the bar. Her singing slowed . . . 'What are you doing to him?'

'You'll see,' Donny sneered. 'Why, you know him?'

Hetty saw Jed shake his head, his lips pursed. 'No,' she said, 'why should I? But I can't sing if a man's suffering like that. I would ask you to untie him.'

'Who's Miss Hoity-Toity think she is?' Harry Holm's mad eyes were fixed on her, taking in her long legs, her low neckline. 'You must be joking, angel.'

And Hetty, in her stage costume and paint, did look angelically decadent. Holm bounded on to the stage and grabbed hold of her.

'That's enough of the singing, sister. You and me got an appointment upstairs.'

'Hold it,' the Kid shouted. 'None of that. She ain't on the menu. I promised her.'

'You what?' Mad Dog roared, twisting her in front of him, and pulling his Colt. 'You think you're the only one got the right to dames? Think again, cowboy. I'm havin' this li'l beaut. You others can fight for her after me. That's fair, ain't it, Dan?'

'Sure,' Hogan drunkenly roared. 'Why not? She's gotta earn her keep.'

Mad Dog dragged the terrified Hetty from the stage, tearing her blouse open so her pale breasts were exposed. Holding her in front of him, an arm around her throat, he dragged her up the saloon stairs.

The Kid's Hopkins and Allen .32 was out, but he didn't dare risk a shot for fear of hitting the girl. Harry Holm snarled and crashed out a shot, spinning the Kid in his tracks, sending him tumbling to the floor.

Mad Dog laughed, picked Hetty up bodily, as if she were a rag doll, and started up the stairs.

'You should not have done that, Harry,' Joe Pizanthia hissed. 'The Kid ... he my friend.' Flame and lead spurted from his carbine, and Mad Dog screamed with agony as the shot snapped his spine. He slithered back down the stairs, Hetty sprawled tumbling over him.

In the confusion Lonesome Annie had slipped behind Jed and cut his bonds. He rolled across the floor and picked up his Smith and Wesson .32 as Donny turned a sawn-off twelve gauge on the Texican and blasted him off his feet.

'Yeah, take that, you greaser rat,' Donny laughed, as the gunsmoke coiled through the saloon to mingle with the girls' screams. 'Whose side you on?'

'How about me?' Jed called, raising the Smith and Wesson as he lay on the floor beside the bleeding Kid.

Donny sent the second barrel of buckshot spraying his way, but it peppered the bottles behind the bar instead, with a crashing of glass. He tottered on his feet for seconds staring with disbelief at the hole in his chest put there by Jed's revolver.

'How about me, punk?' Dan Hogan roared, drawing his Remington. 'You feeling lucky?'

'You're mine, Hogan,' Jed whispered. 'I been waiting a long time.' But when he tried to fire the .32 it jammed . . .

The massive slug smashed through the wooden wall of the bar by his head as Jed rolled aside. When he looked up the hairy Gorgon was swaying on his bowed legs. He clawed at his back where a 9mm. slug was embedded. Another, and another spat out, until he sank, flailing, to his knees.

'Looks like I arrived just in time,' Bill Lawson said, pushing through the door. He thudded four more slugs into Hogan, who finally gave a huge groan and subsided on to the floor. 'Anybody else for tennis?'

Pigeon-toed Sal came up from behind the bar, a wagon spoke in her hand. She cracked Bill hard across the head and he went down. 'I'm with the bad guys,' she grinned.

'Yeah, me too.' Della picked up the Krug and covered them. 'Let's take what there is and get outa here.'

Jed Long stepped over, twisted the Krug from her grip. 'I'm sorry, Della. That's empty and you're not going anywhere. I'm a sworn-in-law-officer. You, Joe and the Kid are all under arrest.'

He kneeled down to study the Kid, who had his hand clutched to his bleeding midriff. 'I warned you to get out when you had a chance. It's too late now.' He took a broken piece of petrified wood from his pocket, matched it with the amulet around his neck. 'That day I saw you by the pool I knew you were my half-brother. It's all right, Kid. I think you'll live.'

The Winnamucca Kid grinned, tossing his hair from his eyes, trying to rest back against the bar. 'Yeah, I knew there was something strange about you. Tell me one thing, did my mother, or our mother, ever speak about me?'

'All the time. It was the hardest thing she ever did, leaving you. She knew that one day we'd meet again.'

The Kid's blue eyes smiled into the blue ones of his half-brother. 'Maybe she'll come and visit me in prison?'

'I think you'll get off light, Kid.' Bill Lawson was rubbing another lump on the back of his head. 'You tried to save Hetty from a fate worse than death.'

The Texican, Pizanthia, was groaning, examining the lead pellet holes in his legs. 'You, too, Joe. You killed Mad Dog. I'm gonna put in a word for you both with the governor. And Della, you tell all you know, I figure they'll go easy on you.'

Hetty had picked herself up, and was watching, covering her breasts, composing herself.

'Couldn't you let them go?'

'No,' Lawson said. 'I play by the book. I'll patch these two up and take 'em back. They'll have to face the judge.'

He went over and gave Dan Hogan a kick to make sure he was dead. 'I'll load these stiffs into the wagon. There's bounty on their heads.'

'There's stolen jewellery upstairs. And this.' She proffered the wad of $250. 'My fee. I can't accept it.'

'Are you OK, Hetty?' Jed was touching her arm. 'What are you going to do?'

'I'm coming with you back to Deadwood, if I may?' Hetty smiled and slipped an arm around his slim waist.

'I'll be the resident singer in Number Forty-four Saloon. We'll make it the dandiest joint there is.'

'How about me?' Lonesome Annie wailed, bursting into tears as she watched the lips of Jed and Hetty tenderly unite. 'Can I come, too?'

'Sure, why not?' Jed smiled over Hetty's shoulder and shrugged. 'Why not? And Frenchie Nell, as well. I guess we'll be needing a coupla dancin' gals.'

Pigeon-toed Sal and Double Barrel Martha scowled. It didn't look like they were invited.

THE END

We do hope that you have enjoyed reading this large print book.

Did you know that all of our titles are available for purchase?

We publish a wide range of high quality large print books including:
Romances, Mysteries, Classics
General Fiction
Non Fiction and Westerns

Special interest titles available in large print are:
The Little Oxford Dictionary
Music Book, Song Book
Hymn Book, Service Book

Also available from us courtesy of Oxford University Press:
Young Readers' Dictionary
(large print edition)
Young Readers' Thesaurus
(large print edition)

For further information or a free brochure, please contact us at:
Ulverscroft Large Print Books Ltd.,
The Green, Bradgate Road, Anstey,
Leicester, LE7 7FU, England.
Tel: (00 44) **0116 236 4325**
Fax: (00 44) **0116 234 0205**

Soon the paddle-steamer would be on its long journey down the Missouri River to St Louis. Now, all Saul Rhymer had to do was to play the last master-stroke of the evening. He looked at the mounting pile of gold and dollar bills and again at the cards in his hand. Then, looking around the table, he produced the deed to the goldmine in Montana. 'Let's play poker!' But little did he know how that journey back to St Louis would change his life so drastically.

THE ARIZONA KID

Andrew McBride

When former hired gun Calvin Taylor took the job of sheriff of Oxford County, New Mexico, it was for one reason only — to catch, or kill, the notorious Arizona Kid, and pick up the fifteen hundred dollars reward the governor had secretly offered. Taylor found himself on the trail of the infamous gang known as the Regulators, hunting down a man who'd once been his friend. The pursuit became, in every sense, a journey of death.

BULLETS IN BUZZARDS CREEK

Bret Rey

The discovery of a dead saloon girl is only the beginning of Sheriff Jeff Gilpin's problems. Fortunately, his old friend 'Doc' Holliday arrives in Buzzards Creek just as Gilpin is faced by an outlaw gang. In a dramatic shoot-out the sheriff kills their leader and Holliday's reputation scares the hell out of the others. But it isn't long before the outlaws return, when they know Holliday is not around, and Gilpin is alone against six men . . .

THE YANKEE HANGMAN

Cole Rickard

Dan Tate was given a virtually impossible task: to save the murderer Jack Williams from the condemned cell. Williams, scum that he was, held a secret that was dear to the Confederate cause. But if saving Williams would test all Dan's ingenuity, then his further mission called for immense courage and daring. His life was truly on the line and if he didn't succeed, Horace Honeywell, the Yankee Hangman would have the last word!

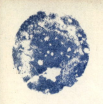

MISSOURI PALACE

S. J. Rodgers

When ex-lawman Jim Williams accepts the post of security officer on the *Missouri Palace* river-boat, he finds himself embroiled in a power struggle between Captain J. D. Harris and Jake Farrell, the murderous boss of Willow Flats, who will stop at nothing to add the giant sidepaddler to his fleet. Williams knows that with no one to back him up in a straight fight with Farrell's hired killers, he must hit them first and hit them hard to get out alive.